WORDS

TO TIE

TO

BRICKS

IN AID OF ST MICHAEL'S HOUSE

WORDS

CREATIVE WRITING FROM CTYI

TO TIE

ANTHOLOGY OF WRITING CLASS, 2013

TO

EDITED BY CLAIRE HENNESSY

BRICKS

CENTRE FOR TALENTED YOUTH IRELAND AT DUBLIN CITY UNIVERSITY

First published in 2013 by
CTYI Press
Centre for Talented Youth Ireland, Dublin City University, Dublin 9

Paperback	ISBN: 978 1 909483 385
eBook – mobi format	ISBN: 978 1 909483 392
eBook – ePub format	ISBN: 978 1 909483 408
CreateSpace edition	ISBN: 978 1 909483 415

Produced by Kazoo Independent Publishing Services
222 Beech Park, Lucan, Co. Dublin
www.kazoopublishing.com

Kazoo Independent Publishing Services is not the publisher of this work. All rights and responsibilities pertaining to this work remain with the CTYI Press.

Kazoo offers independent authors a full range of publishing services. For further details visit www.kazoopublishing.com

Cover design by Andrew Brown
Printed in the EU

Foreword

WORKING AS THE DIRECTOR OF an organisation that celebrates the potential of high-ability students can be a humbling experience when I realise that there are teenagers, and quite often also younger children, who are in many ways smarter than I will ever be. The book that you are reading now further reinforces this opinion.

CTY Ireland is a place where young people who excel in different academic and creative areas get a chance to meet other students of similar ability and hopefully share some common ground. The outcome of this programme regularly exceeds our highest expectations. The work produced is of the highest standard as students get a chance to work at their own pace and engage fully with subjects that are of interest to them. Socially, friendships are made and these can often be lifelong connections.

It has been my privilege to work for this organisation for the past 20 years (yes, that is older than the eldest of the contributors to this book) and over 50,000 students have passed through the doors of CTY Ireland in that period. One of the main goals of the organisation is to challenge academically talented students at a level appropriate to their ability rather than their age. This book allows us to turn this potential into something real.

I'm delighted that any profits from this book will go to St Michael's House that does such great work with people who have intellectual disabilities. With the headquarters across the road from us here at Dublin City University it seems the perfect fit for this book.

Finally I would like to congratulate all the contributors to this book, our fantastic CTY Ireland students and in particular a great former student, the teacher Claire Hennessy. Claire, your dedication to this project makes it worth at least a shortlist for the Booker prize.

Enjoy the book.

Colm O'Reilly
Director
CTY Ireland

Notes from the Authors

To the unprepared reader – We promise there are explanations. We're just not including them, and you should probably be grateful.

To the prepared reader – Please refer to the previous point. You cannot possibly be prepared.

To the parents – Look at what you've released upon the world. Also, we don't need counselling, in case you were wondering.

To the siblings – I'm in a book. Take that. Also: All the mean bits are inspired by you. Congratulations.

To the friends – I hope you remain so after you read that one piece. You know the one.

To the pets – Good money was probably spent on this book. Stop eating it.

To the acquaintances – This is probably more than you wanted to know.

To the teachers – I told you I was special.

To the haters – Don't hate the poet, hate the poem.

To our sworn enemies, the philosophy students – We have a book, you don't exist. Who's the winner here?

To the romantic partners – We swear this is not about you. Unless you want it to be. In which case, it totally is. XOXO

To the ex-romantic partners – This is all about you. Unless you want it to be, in which case it isn't.

To the future romantic partners – This isn't as bad as it looks. By the way, if you find a poem tied to a brick and a broken window in your front room, don't be alarmed. It's a sign of affection, we swear.

To our fellow pathetic writers-to-be – Look how much you can do. Keep your chin up. We're all terrible together. Also, group therapy could be fun.

To the CTYI staff – Thanks for taking a chance on us. We hope you're not crying.

To the world – Whoops. Our bad.

Lots of love, Anthology of Writing Class 2013
xoxox

Anthology of Writing 2013

LIST OF CONTRIBUTORS

Catherine Bowen

Amy Campbell

Sean Ceroni

Grace Collins

Samuel H. Doyle

Andrew Duffy

Caelen Feller

Conor Kelleher

Hannah-Rose Manning

Carol McGill

Orla McGovern

Anna Mulligan

Hannah O'Boyle

Emma Shevlin

Cahal Sweeney

Instructor: Claire Hennessy
Teaching assistant: Emily Collins

Heavy Heart

Emma Shevlin

~~I'm writing this to show you~~
I'm writing this to say
That what I feel inside me,
It just won't go away.

I find it weighs me down,
~~It burns just like a fire.~~
The mass of my emotions,
The density of my desire.

I've found a way to let you know
How much I love you, dear.
Forget the window,
Treasure the brick,
That you find lying here.

I still remember how you take your coffee in the morning

Hannah O'Boyle

There are still crumbs on the desk
from that cake you bought me
when my favourite uncle died
and I was barely eating.

The carpet is still worn
from the time you tried
to teach me how to dance,
and I stepped on your toes.

The petals have fallen
from the flowers you gave
the last time you smiled at me.
I guess that means something.

I still have your pillow.
I hope you don't mind.
(I'm sorry.)
(Come back.)

Success

GRACE COLLINS

I'VE NEVER BEEN SUCCESSFUL. But I have this idea of what it feels like.

Imagine a world. A world where everything is possible. Anything you can dream is a reality, nightmares are a myth, pain an old wives' tale. People don't get old and die so no one is ever burdened with loss. Everyone knows this. They know that the idea of something not existing is the only thing that is impossible. And the consequence of everything is different from here. They are good consequences because bad actions cannot be done.

And today, on this day, people feel something. They don't know what, but they can feel something great in the air. It's pumping throughout their bodies, each step bringing them one step closer to it. No one knows why though. They don't question it but soon they will.

And you, you are the exception to all of this. You know of things that aren't real. You know that not everything you dream is real but you don't care, not one bit. You know that consequences are not always good because bad actions will hurt. And you know that sometimes people die, and it hurts to lose them. You know that soon things will change in this world. And do you want to know what else you know? You know that you are the cause of this greatness and you know that soon, everyone will know this, but it will be too late.

You see, you're in this big old city. Hundreds of people all around. Buildings that mark the wonderful civilizations before cover the ground. You are standing on the top of the tallest, oldest building; you feel no fear, you feel no bravery. You feel nothing. You simply exist. And standing on this height you can see everyone and everything and you can see how they feel the unknown greatness. And if you focus a little bit, you can feel all their emotions, you can feel the happiness and the joy and you feel every emotion at once and you know all these things and you step to the edge of the building.

And you turn your back on the city.

You take a breath.

And you do not jump. You let go.

Such a simple thing to do and yet it has taken all this time. Suddenly you know that the people know and for the first time in your life you are doing something different.

I imagine the feeling of success as not the feeling of hitting the ground, not of letting yourself drop but the feeling in between.

The feeling of falling and the feeling of knowing and the feeling of feeling. And the feeling of doing more than just existing.

That is success.

Even Now, Even Here, Beautiful

Conor Kelleher

In a world where nothing is beautiful,
And if it were, it would be obscured by the black
And by the tint of your gas mask.
The world had long begun to melt.
The planet enveloped by a toxic fog.
A life now not of colours, but of shapes

And on a high hill, are our shifting shapes.
We can't remember anything bright or beautiful,
And so we journey through the fog,
To see if there's anything to be seen that isn't black.
The liquid landscape around us is devoted to the melt.
Or what I can see of it, anyway, through my mask.

The gas means you cannot remove the mask,
And so we've forgotten our faces' shapes.
I think of how little we know of each other, and I begin to melt.
If I could see you, I know you would be beautiful.
All we are outside, silhouettes against black.
All we are inside, twisting fog.

But maybe we should be thankful for that fog,
And the limitations of the mask.
Do we want to see what's blocked by blankets of black?
Do we want those defined shapes?
Maybe the ignorance and blank bliss is beautiful.
My eyes begin to melt.

But we run, even as we melt.
We will find our treasure in the fog,
Even if that treasure is less than beautiful.
Brand new scars mark my mask,
A record of where we've been, and of the shapes
Of what we've carved for ourselves from the black.

There are whispers in the black,
Fixed figures that live in the melt.
We hide from their defined shapes.
I love you, I promise, no matter what happens in this fog.
I love you and I love your gas mask.
It's all fantastically beautiful.

In the black, you slip through the fog.
And the melt devours you through your mask.
I see your gasping faces' shapes. Even now, even here, beautiful.

A Summer's Evening

Carol McGill

IT'S BEEN A SWELTERING DAY, moving slowly into an exhausting, hot night. It's been a day when the sun softens the world with heat and paints everything with gold, a day when all there is to be done is lie in the shade fanning yourself with a napkin, a day to spend sucking at ice lollies or eating strawberries or twisting your hair in your hand so it doesn't stick to the back of your neck.

It's at sunset on a day like this that you come home.

❧

Though it was a day for doing nothing, we did everything.

I took the kids down to swim in the river. When we got back to the house, I let them run on the grass in the garden to dry off. For a while I chased them, laughing hysterically and tickling them, but then the heat got the better of me and I went inside. It was too hot to cook so I made a sort of salad for dinner. I watched through the window as the children chased each other, collapsed with fatigue, and chased once again.

After I called them in we ate the makeshift salad with bread and butter. We drank lots of lemonade and ate lots of ice cream. I took them on a walk to the meadow and told them to be very, very quiet and not to move at all, because then we'd see the rabbits. We wandered home through the dusk and they put on their pyjamas. Becky pulled her nightshirt over her head but then stripped off immediately because she was too hot, so I opened all the windows in their room and let them splash cold water on their faces. I told them a story. When I go back to check on them now they're asleep, but the blankets are in a heap on the floor.

Leaving the back door open, I go outside. It's cooling down out here, despite getting stuffier in the house. The shadows are growing longer and the gold light is fading to give way to night. I walk down the garden and lean on the back gate, watching the sunset. And then

I see you.

You take your time coming up the lane that runs by the back of the house. You're very close before I see your face and I know for sure that it's you. Long before that I become very conscious of how faded the flowers are on the summer dress I'm wearing, of how tangled my hair is and how dirty the soles of my feet are, because it had been too hot for shoes all day. When I see that it's you I feel dreamlike. Not that I think I'm asleep – I know it's real and that's what makes it a dream.

When you finally reach me you stop so there's nothing between us but that rusty gate. This was where you'd always kissed me goodnight. This was where the best kind of silence had always replaced the best kind of words. This was where you'd looked in my eyes and promised never to do what you'd done. This was where I'd waited for you every night, for all of the first year you were gone.

Today, I wait for you to break the silence.

But you don't. You look past me, up the garden towards the house that was our home, with a sort of longing in your eyes.

I wonder if you know about your lighter lying on my dressing table, and how I used it that one time I tried to smoke, after everyone claimed it'd help me relax. I wonder if you know about the way I kept buying your favourite tea bags for months. I wonder if you know how guilty I felt after I replaced those yellow curtains you picked out. If you know how I jumped down my sister's throat when she sat in your chair on her visit. How I had to stop the clock because the ticking drove me mad. How much I cried after giving away your clothes. I wonder if you know how I broke all the china in the house after you were gone.

I wonder if you know just how angry I was.

But I'm doing well. I keep on telling myself I'm doing well. The pain is still there but I'm learning to live with it without hurting too much, and I can manage almost a day without thinking of you. I met a nice guy at the meeting in the town hall, Michael he was called, and he invited me out for coffee and gave me flowers. He's been round a few times, and the kids like him. Max climbed all over him and Becky sat on his knee and looked up at him with round, shy eyes. He tried to kiss me once, I turned my face away so he got my cheek. But I've been thinking about it ever since and maybe next time I'll let him.

Shouldn't you be the first one to speak? I don't know what it is you're here to say.

You touch my face. Your hand is familiar to me. And it's so much better than fantasies or tear-soaked sheets or nights filled with silence.

'It's time to let me go,' you whisper. I shake my head.

'Yes it is. It's time,' you insist, your voice soft. 'You've been holding on to me and I've been holding onto you. But we're both ready. It's time.'

'You promised you'd never leave me,' I choke out. I think I'm crying.

'You know I had no choice,' you remind me gently. How have I managed for so long without you to remind me of things? 'You know it was my time to die. Come on now. You're ready. You can do it. You can let me go.'

I cry. And finally I nod. You lean forward and kiss my mouth. I close my eyes. When I open them there's nothing but the sunset and my fingers stroking thin air.

A Gentleman's Guide To Playing With Your Food

Anna Mulligan

Don't break her; bend her.
Twist her mind back like a finger
And when she begins to drain of colour
Take away her light – slowly,
Like cutting hair – in increments,
Just a little at a time, so one day
She will look in the mirror
And not know herself
Without you.

Don't let her snap – be careful.
Tears are sloppy; keep it to broken sleep.
Limit your effects to restlessness
And self-doubt. Let her see things;
She will lie to herself
For you.

Don't let her starve – feed her
With controlled portions of affection,
Little things:
Careless gestures, hands on hands,
Meaningless glances.
She will use them
To forgive you.

You must never let her see more
Than she can deny to herself
When she tosses
In the night.

Flight

SAMUEL H. DOYLE

One door remained
To be breached.
I lunged for it
The lock shattering
into diamonds and prisms
of enchanting rainbows,
a spectrum unchecked.

I stepped through.

A fantastic gravity pulling
My leaden legs
To the edge.
Some deadly desire forcing my footsteps.
I hung above a crystal precipice,
Crevasses promised
A blissful fall.

I dived off.

My arms opened
Wide like a boiling ocean
Of emeralds and sapphires.
I plunged deeper
Through swirling fogs
Of lavender
Shrouding the treacherous lows.

I unfurled my wings
And flew.

A Broken Us

AMY CAMPBELL

IT IS THREE O'CLOCK IN the morning when I get the call. I pick up on the third ring, like I always do, although we both know I was waiting by the phone. 'Where are you?' I ask; no need for pleasantries. You and I have danced to this music for so long now that I move on autopilot, stepping in time to a song that only we can hear.

'Outside,' you choke, and although I register the tears in your voice, I don't question them, because I lost my curiosity a long time ago.

I open the door, even though I don't want to, and you fall into the dimly lit hallway that used to be called ours. As soon as I flick the switch on the lamp, I regret it; the light lifts the shadows from your face and illuminates bruises, scars and tears that I don't want to see.

There is a fresh cut on your temple, and if you notice the blood running down your cheek, you don't show it. You drop the empty bottle to the ground, and I flinch as it shatters on the wooden floor. I busy myself cleaning the wound on your head and sweeping away the shards of broken glass because it is easier than looking into your empty eyes.

I lead you to the bedroom, as has become routine. You never comment on the blanket that has taken up permanent residence on the armchair and the untouched sheets in our bedroom, never ask why I leave a perfectly good double bed empty every night you're not here. Maybe you know that it is too painful for me to sleep in our space without you. Maybe you just don't notice. You slide between the sheets of the bed that used to be ours but isn't even mine anymore, like nothing has changed.

I don't know how you do it. You act as if the last year never happened and although I wish more than anything that it hadn't, I can't. I can't wake up here with you and find it had been nothing more than a bad dream like you always used to complain of. So I don't speak. Neither do you.

You pull me in like you do every time and although I resist at first, we both know where this is heading. We fall onto our usual sides of the bed, me in a pencil skirt, blouse and blazer from work, you in old jeans, a torn t-shirt and a familiar leather jacket that smells like cigarette smoke and alcohol and your cologne. It is so painfully similar, yet nothing is the same. I know that in the morning I will watch you sneaking out, gathering your clothes from the floor and trying not to wake me. I will pretend to sleep. It's just easier that way.

When I go downstairs I will be able to smell the coffee and see the cup in the sink. You will have taken two of the aspirin that I have started to leave out for you, like a child laying out cookies and milk for Santa Claus. And come night time, you will greet me again with a phone call or a knock on the door and I will get you, wherever you are, and allow you to fall into my arms and pull me into what was once our sanctuary. It might not be tomorrow; I'm never quite sure when it will be. Do you know that I don't go out anymore for fear you'll call and I'll miss it?

I sit in my chair although yours is bigger, watching the phone, willing it to ring and wishing that it wouldn't. I fall asleep there on the nights that you don't call. It's the same old game as always, me taking care of you. I was happy like that; I could have done it forever. You were the one who walked away. You were gone with nothing more than a brief 'it's not working', a rough apology and a pre-packed suitcase.

I knew the first time you slammed the door that you would be back. And I knew the first time the phone rang at three a.m. that you would never fully leave. You would reach for me night after night, and I would reach back, driving to wherever you were two or three times a week, if that was what you needed. Because you never stopped needing me, the same way I never stopped loving you.

☙

When I wake up to the familiar empty bed, I do not feel anything. It is not the first time, nor will it be the last, because you can't stop coming back to a broken us any more than I can stop welcoming a broken you back into a defeated embrace.

Deep

CAELEN FELLER

Out of sight,
Out of comfort,
Bobbing in the sea.
The waves here are gentle,
But their nature is to engulf.

This water is deep,
Enriched by the lives of all creation,
Their history runs in every current.
Yet none have dived deep enough
To see this ocean's floor.

Sinking here is easy.
There are many currents,
Unseen, that clutch at me.
They pull me down, deeper.

Others float and sink.
Caught up in these waves,
They never think to struggle.
Yet simply are pulled along,
And eventually,
The water will drag them down.

When I dive,
And the currents take me,

I see such depths.
Before the breath I took
To sustain me runs out,
I see another world.

The blood of all history runs here,
Diluted in the water.
I swim through it all,
And still continue.

But when the air runs out
And water takes its place,
I always float back to the surface.
Bobbing in the water again.

Home

SEAN CERONI

There is nothing more sinister
Than a comfortable prison.

Yellow

Grace Collins

YELLOW IS HOW A YOUNG boy feels on his first day, in a new place where dreams come true. It's that hopeful giddiness that forces its way into your brain, taking up all your thoughts. It can be comforting, like when you run a bath at the perfect temperature and you lower yourself into it and allow your mind to wander over people you say you don't care for but deep down they mean the most to you.

It's not awkward small talk and pretending that you weren't just staring at a certain someone. It's easy conversation and hearing lovely people laugh at things that aren't that funny. It's your first kiss that you then ran away from and have been embarrassed about ever since. It's the fragile, flirty, nervous, silly relationship you have with someone before you label it and crush what the two of you once shared.

It's knowing that there is someone who for some strange reason still cares for you and is worried about you and realises that there is something wrong although you won't admit it, not even to yourself. It's being cared about. It's seeing that after all you have done you still have someone there.

It's getting a hug that's warm and smells good and lasts just a little bit too long. And finding that perfect place for your hands around someone's neck when they hold you. It's horrible dancing to really bad music but not caring who's watching. And it's doing cartwheels in the rain just because you can.

It's getting a letter you never expected, with that same old messy scrawl that labels the front of a book as being important to you because a wonderful person took time to write it for you. It's saying goodbye to a place where you have had so many good memories, not because you have to, but because you have finally come to peace with saying goodbye. It's seeing that everything that you've ever wanted wasn't actually for you and you were only working towards it and saying it because it fits the mould of what people want for you.

Yellow is having conversations planned in your head only to have the other participant not follow the script in the best way possible. Yellow is giving the perfect gift to someone on their birthday. And knowing that somewhere, you're crossing someone's mind right now.

Yellow is rereading your favourite parts of books and taking the last sip of tea from a cup: savouring its taste and letting it warm you from the inside out. It's listening to an album from start to finish and not realising that there's no more music flooding your ears. It's waking up in the middle of the night and watching the moon, wondering who else is up.

It can be sad, it can be going for a walk in the dark and then calling a friend from a random phone booth to ask them to come pick you up, only to cry when they get there. It can be fake and phony and putting up a brave front. And sometimes you need that front because it'll help you to know what the dream is like and it makes you want it more.

Someone's going to find the crack, so be careful. But cracks are made to be picked at. For someone to come along and uncover your greatness. To pick you up, cuddle you close and tell you it's gonna be okay. That's yellow too.

My End

EMMA SHEVLIN

When I leave
I want to take the words that fueled my soul.
The friendship.
The romance.
The love.
The fiction.

When I leave
I want to hear the melodies that brought me through.
Ecstatic music.
Heartbreak music.
Poignant music.
Our music.

When I leave
I want to be crowded by those who helped me along.
My family.
My friends.
My enemies.
My people.

When I leave
I want to have mountains of memories I have built up in my time.
Recite them.
Share them.
Document them.
Remember them.

When I leave
Don't ever stop feeling.
Continue to fear.
Continue to conquer.
Continue to love.
Continue to live.

My ending should not prompt yours.

An Introduction To Me

Amy Campbell

NOBODY IS PERFECT, BUT we will all die trying. I am not perfect, and am able to accept the fact that I never will be. Perfection has never been something I strived for. Perfect people aren't real, they aren't interesting. And I like to believe that my flaws are what make me who I am.

I may not be the prettiest girl you know. My eyes are too far apart, my nose is too wide, my hair goes fuzzy in the rain. I may not be the smartest girl that you know. I am proud to bring home a report card with mainly B's, I don't know the surface area of the earth, I never quite understood long division. I may not be the nicest girl that you know. I say things without thinking, don't say thank you often enough, forget the manners my parents spent fifteen years teaching me. I may not be the strongest girl that you know, or the most popular, or the best at drawing, dancing or science. I will never be a professional footballer, or any footballer for that matter. I can't describe myself in adjectives, lay out my personality in words and definitions from the dictionary. Because I am none of them. And at the same time, I am all of them.

I have always used words to express my feelings. I text my friends about my day, share my thoughts on Facebook, jot down my life into the journals I keep. I write songs and stories and poems to describe the feelings I couldn't possibly explain. And yet I cannot describe myself using only words. I can only tell you what I am not. Perfect. What am I? Everything else.

I can be loud, I can sing and yell and make crazy noises until my voice is hoarse. And yet at the same time, I can savour the hours alone when I am lost within myself, in a dreamland that only I have ever been to. I can be happy, I can run around the school singing and laughing and proclaiming that we live in a wonderful world. And I can have days when my eyes are red, and I choke on my words and I want nothing more than to be hugged and told that everything will be all right. I am ambitious and driven and enthusiastic, but some days my answer to every question is, 'because I can't be bothered.'

I laugh with people, I laugh at people. I talk to people, I talk about people. I dream of the life I would live if I won the Lotto, the things I would say if I was brave enough, the celebrities I fall in love with. I dream about the perfect world, where there is no war or poverty or death. I am just like any normal teenager. There's nothing special or extraordinary about me, nothing that sets me apart from all the rest. I am just me. And I cannot be described in four paragraphs. I've known me for sixteen years and I still surprise myself every day.

So if you want words to describe me, try all of them. Because that's what I try to be. Everything. I want to be friendly and funny and creative and talented and smart and pretty and loyal. I want to change the world some day, even just a little bit. I want to be the best that I can be at everything I do. But I'll settle for being me. Because in the end, that's all I can be.

&

Silence

ORLA MCGOVERN

Silence condenses, squeezes,
Makes the profound more profound.
Its pressure creates complex
Paintings of the simplest sounds.

The silence after a song
Is when the emotion hits,
As everyone hurts and feels and cries
While the silence bends and shifts.

It brings couples close ... closer
And crashes them to an end.
Silence is sad, solemn and lonely
But the lonely make good friends.

Made of Glass

CAELEN FELLER

It's said that hearts are made of glass,
That glass will shatter in the end.
That someone will make a crack.

And this crack will creep along,
Until the seal on a heart is broken,
Ruby droplets gathering along its length.

But glass can be collected,
Melted down, formed again,
We can always have a new beginning.

Broken glass is a dangerous thing,
Slitting our hands as we mend it.
Opening old wounds to bleed again.

But with you,
I can just sweep the glass away
And forget.

I don't need my broken heart,
When I have yours.

I Did It

Andrew Duffy

I DID IT. THE ROOM filled with the stares of pure disgust and, in some cases, sheer savage animalistic rage. All I could say was 'what?' They cried, they screamed the whole house into Hades and blew the neighbourhood to the outer reaches of the galaxy. All I could do was laugh at their whining, their misery at the smallest of things. An action that in the grand scheme of the universe means absolutely nothing. A decision on a speck of dust on the third rock from the sun in the only solar system known to possess life.

It means nothing to me; I have done no wrong, committed no offence. Only in the eyes of my peers have I committed an atrocity to rival the worst violations of the Geneva Convention. But I didn't know. I simply had no clue, not a notion of what I was condemning myself to.

I am however not sorry. There are no apologies for this. For a man who commits no wrong should not have to apologise.

I genuinely don't care that it was the last biscuit.

Slammed Receiver

Anna Mulligan

I really did love you, you know.
Like sunlight on water.
Like a shoelace
Caught
In escalator blades.
Like I was going to stay
For the rest of my life.

I knew your voice
Better than mine –

But it's time.

Stop calling.

Fading Spirit

Samuel H. Doyle

It was hard to return.
You wouldn't believe so but ...
I had memories of this place   happy memories,
But I don't recognise it, they have to be mistaken.
No, maybe it's just different ... older ...   weaker.
'Take care, dem rocks are fierce shlipp'ry.' I'm reminded,
I'm nearly as feeble as this place ... my place once.

It's too quiet, unnatural in the countryside ...   eerie.
I comment, get hushed,
'Ach sure, dey left wen dee city yolks went a quarr'in.'
Yes ...   yes,   they must be right, scared away all the life.
Still I wish I could hear it again,
The sweet chirp and song of the birdies,
The distant howl of the hounds and hunt,
The faint rustling of the pheasants in McCullom's meadow.
Ahh, that was being alive ...   no more.

Oh God what ruin, a house they say ...   my house,
No, this is no one's home.
Yet, if I search deeply, imagine briefly, I see it there.
Those whitewashed walls, crumbling ...   collapsing,
Keeling over like a stranded trawler on Nolan strand,
Once stood tall, no pride but height.
These walls were my support,
My lifetime cradle, strong as I became,

Supportive like the person I once was.
These small walls were my haven and shelter,
A simple sanctuary throughout all troubles.

But with time they fell.

The Second

(an excerpt from a novella)

Anna Mulligan

YOU WILL NOT WANT TO go to the party where you meet her. You will fight it; you will text your friends and tell them you're busy. You will set up a night for yourself; textbooks stacked up, reruns queued on your computer, three cans of Coke waiting at the edge of your desk to swoop in and tune you up. You will tell yourself that tonight is a perfectly fine night for staying in.

But you will look out the window when you ought to be drilling verbs and the indigo evening will seep in under the sill and the tree out front will whisper to you. You will feel the little tug in your stomach of missing memories being made, the ghost of regret future, and you will know that the textbook mountain will not be scaled this evening, because you will hear the pulse of the music. The vibrations will break into your home and make your body second-guess you, and you will know that you can't stay in tonight.

You won't want to go. You won't want to get up from your chair, but the feel of it – of something happening, of being on the sidelines – will be too much for you, and you will go. You will straighten yourself out and refuse to change because it's not like you're staying long or anything and you will leave your things on the desk like you might get back to them – even if you know that tomorrow, when you see them there, you will feel like you let them fall to ruin, like you are at a museum and they are a statue missing half a face and a left arm – and you will go.

You will stand up and pause, listening to the revelry unravelling next door, considering and reconsidering, but in the end, you will go.

You will pad carefully down the stairs even though your parents are away for the weekend recuperating from something or other, and your sister is spending the night at her boyfriend's and you're covering for her because she said please and you're practically Jesus – it won't matter that the house is too empty to judge you. It will still feel illicit somehow, leaving your desk for the unknown. When you catch yourself sneaking, you will hesitate, torn between the comfort of your planned evening and the siren call of next door, but you will go, because you blow your friends off enough as it is and the verbs will wait and you want more than a queue of Cokes in single file and you keep missing things and you know your verbs just fine anyway.

You will shut the front door gently, looking away from the monstrous youth of next door to the rest of the street, sleeping almost-soundly in sepia streetlight, quaint as can be. It will remind you of playing chasing there, and some part of you will shrink back from the idea of turning from it to the house next door. You will almost turn back, almost leave this street to itself and go back to your books, but you'll hear the undeniable rhythm of how young you are from behind you, and you will turn and go to the party.

It will be like every other house party. You will have your eyes open for your friends; you will know they'll be pleased to see you and even more pleased to ply you with alcohol and loosen you up, but they will not appear. You will look around, realising that you have come just a little too late to properly partake, that you have come to it as a spectator now, always a little too sober to ever catch up to the vocational insanity of it all. You will feel the sinking swallow of regret as you pick up a plastic cup and pour yourself a small glass of something unpleasant. You will look around at the assembled revellers, sprawled in various states of intoxication and youth, engaged in all manner of activities that are entirely different kettles of fish when sober, and you will knock back your drink in one go, wishing you hadn't come but not enough to leave.

You will wander through the sea of limbs, wondering often how so much can be squashed into a house not different from your own, and though you will see acquaintances – the host, the guy you sit behind in History, the barista from the coffee shop you go to during study breaks – you will not be able to make eye contact. You will remember why you don't go to parties – why the siren call is just that, and why you ought to listen to your instincts. You will wonder if you will ever really feel like one of a group like this – if any amount of alcohol or free time or success or failure will ever make you feel like you belong in this picture.

You will whip yourself into a cantankerous frenzy and almost leave there and then. In fact, you will be turning to leave when you see her.

She will be in the emptiest room, almost alone. She will fit into the landscape like she was painted there; she will look like she belongs when she sips her cup, smoothly, like this is not her first time at the rodeo, and something in the stretch of her neck as she finishes the drink and the way it makes her straightened dark hair betray itself into waves will enchant you, and you will be caught.

You will freeze where you are for a second, two, lost in the hubbub of drunkenness and noise, eyes fixed on her. You will not be able to look away.

You will walk towards her. Your body will be suddenly unwieldy and clumsy; you will feel graceless, walking towards her, knowing that her shining dark eyes might at any moment be upon you. You will mess with your hair, adjust your clothes, curse your inadequate frame and build and body. You will want to leave, to leave this dreamlike avenue of action unsullied; but she will look across the room, tossing her hair gently to look out of the black mirror-like window, and you will be enthralled, and unable to do anything but move towards her.

You will think she doesn't see you. It will seem impossible that someone like her could ever have their eyes caught on someone like you.

But she will speak to you.

'Who are you?' she will ask, softly, like you are alone together. Her voice will burn you to a crisp in the best way and you will take the last step towards her until your bodies are feet from each other.

You will know that it's your name she wants, but it will feel like an invitation to turn your secrets out for her, and you will be willing, so willing.

'Kit,' you will say, and your throat will catch on it. You will be embarrassed, but not enough to move away.

She will smile like you have told her a secret. 'Kit,' she will repeat, and her voice will make it worth owning. 'Are you from around here?'

The words will sound exotic and elegant in her voice. For a moment, you will forget where you live and what you have been doing with the last seventeen years of your life. You will blink once, twice, in the silence.

There will be noise all around you, general noise, movement and conversation and music, but you will not hear it.

'Next door.' Your voice will let you down; it will sound too much like falling short.

She will be leaning against a battered brown piano pushed up against the wall. You will be grateful for it, because it will stretch her pale form along its length and make it exquisitely harder to breathe.

She will notice you looking. She will look down at the piano, generously assuming you are examining the golden curls of decoration on the piano face and not the way her dark blue dress tightens at her waist and suggests hips and legs and other things hidden by the curtain of her dark shining hair. Your eyes will catch more than once on that hair; the occasional subtle wave, shining in the not-light, almost close enough to touch.

'Do you play?' she will ask, her head tilting charmingly. You will be charmed.

'A little,' you will lie. No matter that you will have a piano stool perpetually overflowing sheet music. No matter that your hands – good for so little, too thin for sports, too long for writing implements – will have worked for years to stretch so wide. You will not want to play for her; she will be too much, she will be more than you can imagine playing for, it would be a concert in Carnegie Hall, playing in front of this girl.

But her eyes will light up, and she will clasp her hands together in delight. 'Play me something!' she will demand, her smile warming you up like candlelight. 'I can't do anything like that. Show me! Play for me!'

You will shake your head. After all, she won't know you at all. Poor playing is endearing when a close friend makes the mistake of showcasing it; strangers do not have such rapport. You won't want to risk it.

But she will play dirty. She will look at you with sparkling eyes and move towards you and look into you and say 'please?' and you will fall to her because you will feel it already.

'What do you want to hear?' you will ask. You will be frantically running through your repertoire, trying to find the perfect fit for this girl. You will want very badly to impress her and have absolutely no idea how.

'A song. Do you sing? You look like you sing. You should sing,' she will say. How she guessed it, you won't know. You have never really looked like a singer. You have quiet looks.

But you can sing – she will have seen it in your reaction; your body will have betrayed you, sided with her. It will not be the last time.

'Sing for me!' she will demand, delighted, and it will be hard to be nervous when her infectious smile is close enough to catch.

And you will fight it for a minute or two, shaking your head as she nods hers, but you will surrender to her, because there will be a light in her eyes you can't bring yourself to deny.

You will purse your lips to keep from smiling and look down. 'I'm no Mozart,' you will mumble as she slides off the piano. Her arms will fold and her eyebrows will rise and you will be able to see her eyes truly for the first time – shadowed in dark powder, lined, but electric – and it will be enough to drive you to slide onto the stool and to push your fingers to lift the smooth dark cover and rest on the white keys.

You will take a breath, and her teeth will bite down on her lower lip, and you will start to play, singing the low melody under the piano, your fingers as nimble and smooth as ever.

None of it will be special. You won't feel anything much, playing for her. Maybe a little squashed flame of a rush, a scrunched-up accordion of excitement, but it will be nothing compared to what you feel when you get to the part you know best and turn to look over your shoulder and see her dancing.

It will be shocking, somehow. You will be at a house party, after all; dancing is a given, along with drinking, general debauchery and someone vomiting somewhere they shouldn't. Dancing shouldn't be so surprising, but it will be. It will be like you have been given a window into something beyond incredible, watching her twist and turn to the music, swaying and setting her cup down on a side table so she can raise her hands to the ceiling. The way she moves will captivate you; how she is able to bring her whole self together to the music and how she can transcend the stepping over of rugs and the presence of side tables and the buzz of other music and other people to be this.

You will wonder if some day this moment will be nothing more than a rehashed summer memory; if the magic will lose its lustre with time. You will ask yourself if you could ever contain enough of her in any record you could keep to stop you forgetting why it can be a good idea to abandon verbs for parties.

Don't worry. This is only the beginning.

With the Birds

CAELEN FELLER

Birds sit on the wire outside.
They can feel the cold.
It has been in the air for years.
Predatory by nature,
It bites them, takes those weakest.

The birds have no warm jumpers,
They have no mittens.
They've lost them, I'm sure.
I think how cold they must be.
I feel it – it chills me as I watch them.

They're only birds.
Not real people, I know.
When a person is taken,
People care.
We watch them as they go.

A frozen bird is surrounded,
By other birds, those who care.
Watching, I am fascinated.
My mind wanders.
I'm with the birds.

My head is in clouds.
It begins to snow again,

The snow covers the bird in a shroud,
Buries it.
I mourn with the birds.

We Regret to Inform You, Madame

Conor Kelleher

Sit,
Ink,
Pen,
Fold,
Envelope,
Send.

Wait.

Receive,
Open,
Read,
Cry,
Crumple,
Toss,
Burn.

Home

GRACE COLLINS

MAYBE, JUST MAYBE, I'LL COME home. In a physical sense I've never left but really I've been gone for years. My body still walks around, smiling and making small talk when needed. But it's hollow and empty; there is no passion in it. You see once upon a time, I heard of these wonderful things and I told myself stories of what would and what could happen if I was brave. I started to feel like I needed to chase these dreams, each sentence drawing me slightly closer to where I thought I should be. And I started to see the dangers of the world and the darkness along the path that laughed an evil laugh, but it intrigued me and I needed to know more. I thought that I could bring back the light that had been so kind to me. The light that had held my hand and made me smile. But in the dark I started to see things in people. It was as if their flaws had been painted onto their front. And it scared me; what if I became like them? But I wanted to know more about them, and how they let this happen, so I kept going.

I asked the dark about the light and the smiles it brought and why people here are afraid of the darkness. And it drew me in, it kissed my lonely lips and filled me with fables and stories and told me what I could be and it made me its lover but all the while it was weighing me down, ready to throw me in for the vultures.

The light tried to warn me. But it all seemed so easy and simple and I thought I was in control. I thought that good things were soon to come. One day my foot got stuck in a root of an old tree. The tree laughed at me for falling and let its roots curl up around my leg, making its way to my torso until it consumed my whole body. Then it squeezed me tighter and tighter, crunching my bones and making my eyes go pop and it didn't stop as I screamed and tried to escape its grasp. But when I stopped trying to break free, it passed me from root to branch until I was at its tallest limb. Here it let me swing like a pendulum, it let the fear of falling grow and grow and then it let that fear grow to hope. And when it knew that I was wishing and dreaming of falling it placed me down gently and let me be. It knew that this was a much worse fate than falling. I continued on my way, being drawn in with hope and idealistic little dreams of what could be.

The road has ended now. I ask my friend the darkness where it is, to help me, and it laughs. And it laughs and laughs and the trees join it and the shadows join them and soon everyone is laughing but me. And I don't understand. And then I see that I have been fading; I'm not the person I started out as. I am the darkness and I am the badness. I am the coldness and I am the fear. I have become all that I was afraid of and that does not make me brave or strong. It makes me weak and fragile. I can see that I could not bring back the light, I've been made feeble by the dark. And I can see now that nothing was real. And what now? Nothing. I am nothing and I shall never return. Maybe I don't want to and maybe I don't deserve to.

Maybe this is my home.

‽

Haiku

HANNAH O'BOYLE

Inkless white paper.
I cannot think of the words
to bring you to me.

To My Redo Button

EMMA SHEVLIN

I don't know how I found you,
Hidden among the trees.
We've started our new journey,
And must follow the gentle breeze.

It carries the pieces with it,
The shards that are my heart,
Over to greener pastures.
I've come back to the start.

A beginning where I am whole,
A canvas awaiting the paint
To give the plain some colour
Even if those hues are faint.

Fly with me among the clouds,
We'll soar and twist and turn.
We'll dance among the shining rays,
Be careful not to burn.

Off to the Right

Emma Shevlin

There's a spark down deep inside,
It pricks as sharp as pins.
It makes me feel alive for once,
Lets me forget my sins.

This feeling rushing through me,
Ignites my every cell
Because for these few minutes
I've broken from the shell.

I'm not the one called stupid.
The little girl known as innocent.
I can be the one you've wanted,
A moment's bliss …

    That has been spent.

Because I am alone again,
The moment has gone by,
But I won't crumble to pieces.
I would not dare to cry.

I am like a jam jar
With the lid screwed extra tight,
Locked up in a cupboard
Somewhere to the right.

I'm better off out of sight.

Dust on the Tracks

Caelen Feller

We see a sea of faces,
Their features pressed against the glass,
Dulled eyes lost in monotonous grey.

We move so fast on this train.
But we must shut the Doors tightly
To keep the faces out.

For an unsettling truth is descending.
The windows are fracturing,
The hinges rusting.

The Doors are opening.
And their fingers are what pull
And pry them apart.

Dust gathers on the tracks,
It catches in the wheels.

Immortal Jellyfish

ANDREW DUFFY

IT'S QUITE ROMANTIC, ISN'T IT – the idea of immortality? The notion that one individual could, in spite of all odds, withstand the test of time and live into infinity. Think of all the glorious wonders you could achieve. You could change the world. Heal it, improve it, teach the countless generations you would live through how to build a utopia. Or you could go down the path of control and domination – due to the lack of knowledge and experience that mortals suffer from, you could easily control the planet for the everlasting duration of your lifespan. You could control anyone; you will certainly encounter enemies but you will also possess the time and knowledge to punish and torture them.

But perhaps the one who suffers the most in your infinite lifespan is you yourself. All that you grow to love and cherish during your time will wither and die while you remain fit and alive. The music that comforts you will only play for several decades. The sports and games you have developed a fondness for will eventually change until they are almost unrecognisable. The languages you acquired during your endless travels will become gibberish in several hundred years. All these vast changes will occur until you are left feeling alone, empty and helpless, adrift in the currents of time. There you will be in a cold ocean of infinity where one can truly say, 'I am alone.' Believe me when I say I know. You don't make friends when you're an immortal jellyfish.

Give It To Me Straight

AMY CAMPBELL

Your eyes wide with the question,
But I don't know what to say.
There's no right way to phrase this,
It wasn't meant to be this way.

Each second we are silent
Drops off of us like rain.
I really should say something,
You must think I'm insane.

I try and fail to make something up,
But to lie you must be calm.
I gibber out the awkward question.
'Oh,' you laugh, 'I am.'

Check the Box

ORLA McGOVERN

'I'm a girl.'
'I'm not.'
'I'm neither.'
'I'm both.'

'I'm Catholic.'
'I'm Protestant.'
'I'm atheist.'
'I don't know.'

'I'm homosexual.'
'I'm straight.'
'I'm asexual.'
'I'm bi.'

I feel like I should know
Which label's mine.

On the Other Hand, Flowers
(An excerpt from a work in progress)

CATHERINE BOWEN

DECLAN SNIFFLED AND WIPED HIS running nose into the blanket wrapped around his shoulders. His damp clothes hung off the fire guard behind him. He sat hunched on the stones of the hearth with his back to the flames. His mother had wanted to run him a bath but he was too stubborn to ever willingly take more than one soak a week, even while shivering. He began to regret this decision as a tickling feeling started to crawl up his throat. He knew he was getting a cold.

The idea of being sick over the weekend irritated him. This occurrence would normally have elicited a feeling of outrage from Declan. Normally, however, there were things to *do* at the weekend.

It had been raining and sleeting continuously for a full week now.

Every lunch and break time, the teachers kept the students locked inside. Not that the girls minded. They giggled and coloured and were generally as annoying as usual. Meanwhile Declan and the other boys clutched their hurleys and pressed their faces mournfully up against the glass of the windows.

By Friday it had reached the point that the boys had run off at the end of school to the field by the river to play. The rain had eased into a drizzle which clung to their jumpers in droplets. The river was close to overflowing and the field was saturated. The ground glistened and a pond had formed by the hedgerow.

They were about to try to brave the sodden earth when Joe's mother found them. The boy was dragged away by the ear while his mother screeched in it. It was a grand total of two minutes before the others were given the same treatment by their own parents.

After Mam had finished reprimanding him, she had left him here to wait until his clothes had dried. Or possibly until he died of boredom. Rose sat opposite him on the couch, writing into her hardback copy. The books from her schoolbag had spilled out around her feet and he could see an old essay covered in little red markings peeking out from her English book.

Declan never wanted to go into secondary school. Homework at the weekend! What kind of monsters would do that?

Any other time he would leave Rose be. If she wasn't talking about some boy with 'dreamy eyes', she was prattling on about makeup and neither were topics he had a smidgeon of interest in. Then again, his trousers were still dripping onto the stones and he was going to collapse if he didn't do *something* soon.

'What's that?' he asked, cutting through the silence.

'Homework,' she replied without raising her eyes. She coughed into the back of her hand and kept writing.

'What kind of homework?'

'I've to write an essay for English.' Her eyes were narrowed in suspicion as she answered. He knew that she was questioning his motives.

'Read it for me,' he requested, flashing a smile. When he was younger, he quickly learnt that little boys with big smiles were generally considered 'cuddly' and 'cute' and had turned his grin into a work of art. The dimples of his cheeks never failed him.

Rose sighed, clearly feeling put upon, but began reading nonetheless.

'There is a sense of anticipation as –'

'What's that mean?'

Her glare was icy and he threw his hands up in surrender.

Rose cleared her throat and started again.

'There is a sense of anticipation as winter ends.

'Snowdrops force their way up through the hardened soil to act as standard-bearers for oncoming forces. The sun begins to linger in the sky each day to watch as legions of daffodils gather. Their bright petals pay tribute to the sunlight.' She seemed quite pleased with her choice of words there and Declan tried not to mock her hand gestures as she spoke. 'A tension builds and animals cautiously venture from their hideaways.

'With the war cry of a bird, it begins. Buds fire open. Frost sweeps over fields at night and chokes the life from new sprouts. Hordes of rabbits,' Rose paused to turn the page, 'pour out from their burrows. An icy wind brings blankets of cloud to keep the grass from growing. After countless battles between flora and frost, the land is painted green. The forces of spring rejoice as their enemy is forced back and finally banished.'

The door opened and Mam leaned through. 'Tea, anyone?'

'No thanks, Mam,' they chanted in reply. She smiled and shut the door, sending a wave of cold air through the room.

Declan shivered once and waited as Rose searched for her place.

'The armies rejoice in their triumph. Grass reaches to the sky in exuberance. Flowers burst open as fireworks of celebration and foxgloves serve as bells of victory. Honey bees are messengers of the good news. The landscape brims with life. Plants stretch and bear fruit for a banquet. The scorching sun now remains astonishingly long in the sky to watch the festivities.

'However, with time its interest fades. The ethereal witness,' – the smug way Rose said ethereal didn't sit well with him – 'grows weary and drifts from sight earlier with every passing day. The warmth it provides slips away and the growth of life slows.

'The lush leaves lose their brilliance. Cold mists flow over hedgerows and cling to the ground each evening. A howling wind warns of an inevitable defeat. As a farewell to a time of plenty, the leaves turn golden and branches hang heavy with nuts and berries.

'Frost returns, hungry for retribution. Soon leaves fall to the enemy and the animals retreat. The trees become dormant, waiting until they can once again reclaim the land.'

Declan frowned, unsure how to feel about the piece. On one hand, it was war, which he liked. On the other, it was about *flowers*. Why ruin the fighting by making it all girly? And if she was going to make it girly, why didn't she just make it all about kittens and rainbows and dresses?

'What do you think?' Rose drawled out, getting up to stoke the fire.

He stuck out his tongue in reply, causing her to roll her eyes and smile as she threw a turf briquette into the flames. She sat back down, switching copies and taking a calculator from the bag at her feet. He returned to checking his trouser legs every few seconds. Why were they taking so long to dry?

Unrequited Love

SAMUEL H. DOYLE

I laboured all night long,
Hunchbacked, hiding in homely robes.
My eyes strained, pupils dilated with the depth of the darkness,
Striving to express the extent of my emotions.

Hurrying hands growing cramped,
Crooked fingers curling and clenched.
The inky nib scratched irregularly
As I scrawled, blotching my page.

My mind loosely rambled onwards
Towards a completion that couldn't come too soon.
A writing wreck, as salty moisture welled
Within weary eyes that craved for release.

Beyond witching hour the cartridge ran dry,
My word-wand's scribblings forced to stall.
Arms thrown back, writhing and grasping at air
Before slamming shut the stained paper sheaves.

A fiery arrow ascending above the hills,
The cheering sun, a candle of hope
Renewing all of Earth's natural splendour.
I rose refreshed; confident and prepared.

Later ... all beliefs found dashed against the wall,
Splattering, smashed on the brutal brickwork.
A labour of love lasting all night long,
And in the end, good for nothing.

The Routine

ORLA MCGOVERN

Wet face,
Racing mind,
Sobbing breaths,
Blade kind.

Quick slash,
Sharp pain,
Short pause,
Blood fain.

The Sense of a Meal

ANDREW DUFFY

I CAN SMELL. IT IS glorious; the delightful aromas liberate me from the mundane. The smell of home fills my nostrils and floods every hole and crevice of my olfactory system with fumes of beauty and grace in the form of a freshly prepared specimen.

I can touch. I rub the edges of its space. With every scrape of my fingers over its form I can feel my bones shake with the delight of the feeling, a moment where my skin freezes and I am completely locked in the embrace of this beautiful object.

I can hear. It is the clatter and banter of those around me, some of whom are too caught up in their socialising to truly embrace the deity in front of them. There are some who take time out of their social lives to enter this world of wonder but tragically only stay for small periods only to return to the dull world of human interaction. Then there is myself, too caught up in my quest for enlightenment to pay the slightest bit of concern to the affairs of the human world.

I can see. It is bright and brilliant, it is a parade of colours marching down towards my eyes, and my eyes open eager to greet the blessed colours of the day. All of the colours melt together to form perfection right before my fortunate eyes.

I can taste. That is the best of all senses, for without it I could not appreciate the true joys of this heavenly item. For without tasting it, one confines themselves to the role of a spectator, unable to participate in the glorious triumphs of this action. Honestly, who wants to eat a dinner they can't taste?

Young Love (Sestina)

SAMUEL H. DOYLE

One night I heard scrabbling paws
In the dark guided by your sensitive nose.
A face appeared framed with light whiskers,
As I ran to you, you began to purr.
In the dark I could see your eyes shine
Simply expressing your love.

The fireside armchair you used to love
Is now torn and scarred by your velvet paws,
The tatters as your memorial shine.
I remember how you sniffed the chair with your nose
Prompting me to laugh with your purr
As I teased your ticklish whiskers.

I still have a picture, your whiskers
Curled up in the style we all love,
I can nearly hear you purr.
There are still mucky marks of your paws
Along the tracks you followed with your nose,
Wet and gleaming, a natural shine.

It's hard to forget how the lamps would shine
Brightly upon your silvery whiskers
Twitching with the movement of your little black nose.
You were the one pet I cared to love
With your tiny cute paws
And the sweet growly purr

As you grew older you wanted to purr
The night away in the moonshine.
You appeared to have no paws
In the dark that concealed your whiskers
That was a sight I used to love
Only given away by your glistening nose.

Years ago you would nuzzle your cute nose
Up against my hand and purr,
Enticing me to demonstrate my love
By stroking your glossy fur until the shine
And luminescent glow of your whiskers
Reflected on your happy pattering paws.

I remember how your nose in the lamplight used to shine,
How your purr reverberated through your cheeky whiskers.
I still keep my love alive though you have stilled your paws.

Bygones

Anna Mulligan

You were just an innocent bystander;
Just watching a foreign movie
Without subtitles.

I'm the one who locked this door
Between us; but a part of me wonders
If you ever even tried the handle.
I can't forget that when I was most alone
I was with you.

You Are Now, Always Have Been, and Forever Will Be an

Conor Kelleher

A is for the AA meeting where you met her.
A is for the attempts she makes to get better.

F is for the friends who don't have a clue.
F is for the fears that they have around you.

T is for the trauma she carries around.
T is for the times when she can't make a sound.

E is for the every day she lives with this.
E is for the ending you wish could exist.

R is for the right words that you never knew.
R is for the reversing you wish you could do.

T is for the trauma you tried to carry around.
T is for the times she couldn't be found.

H is for the hurt that she knows she's dished out.
H is for the hope she has, too quiet to count.

O is for the optimism that got you so far.
O is for optional: that's all that you are.

U is for the understanding, you don't know what it's for.
U is for the ultimatums, why not make some more?

G is for the good times you'll never achieve
G is for the going. Great. Leave.

H is for the hurt that you know you've dished out.
H is for the hopes you have, too few to count.

T is for the trauma left lying around.
T is for timeless: you'll never be refound.

~

Florabotanica

Sean Ceroni

Take me to the forest,
Where all the flowers grow,
Cover me in lilies,
And leave me there alone.

Smile

AMY CAMPBELL

MY REFLECTION IN THE MIRROR greets me as I walk in, a silent reminder that after all that I have lost, I still have myself. It's crazy, because that's the one thing I really hadn't wanted to keep. There is a moment of hesitation, a few fleeting seconds when I almost think that my life is worth something. Then I laugh. It punctures the silence in the room like a needle in a balloon. Who am I kidding?

With the first drop of blood that falls from my wrist, I breathe a sigh of relief, because finally I feel something. After months of fake smiles and self assurances that I am happy, this is something real. The blood pumping out of my wrist shows me that I am a person. I'm crying now, all the tears I've been holding in for months. And then, using the scalpel stolen from the science lab, I draw more blood.

I look at myself in the mirror. Mascara down my cheeks, messy blonde hair, dirt and blood on my dress. This is the furthest from perfect I've ever been. I make another incision on my arm, deeper this time. I am frustrated, ready for this to be over. Finally, I feel myself getting dizzy. My eyelids begin to flicker, and I lose the strength in my legs. As I sink down, my grip on the scalpel loosens, and it clatters to the floor. I don't need it anymore anyway. Not where I am going. I am leaving high school behind; all the bullying, the drama, the betrayal. My eyes close for the last time. My heart rate becomes more uneven. This is it. At last.

I hear the door of the bathroom open, and then I hear a scream. A cry for help. More people coming. They are getting closer, feeling for a pulse, calling an ambulance. One or two of them tell me to hold on, not to die. But they can't fool me. I am on my way to my better place, nearly there now. They won't be able to catch me.

I hear the battle cry of a siren in the distance. That was quick. But now my time is nearly up. I will outrun them all. Slowly, all the noises begin to fade out. The laborious beats keeping me alive slow down. I am finally done. All I can see is darkness; all I can hear is silence. I am coming home. The world slows around me, until it is nothing but an imperfect blur filled with imperfect people like me. Maybe that's all it has ever been. I feel my heart beat one last time, and then it gives up.

I smile.

Cyborg

ORLA MCGOVERN

External, jerky and stiff,
Internal, squishy and sad.

Soaked To My Blood

EMMA SHEVLIN

The rain makes up
For the tears I lack.
The love I once had
Will not come back.
He ruined it for
The rest of the boys.
I've put it away
With all of my toys.

I've locked love up
And swallowed the key.
Now only rain
Beats down on me.
Right down through,
Soaked to my blood,
I make my way
Home through the mud.

This path was once
As clear as glass.
I hope that soon
The pain will pass,
So my life can heal
And my heart can escape,
To be held by a boy
And not by an ape.

Frosty Windshields, Glass & Cellar Doors

CAELEN FELLER

Scuttling.
No light.
No shadows.
Just Dark.

Slipping.
No warnings.
No help.
Just Dark.

Watching.
I know you.
I know
You are there.

Scratching.
Glass shattering.
Scattering.
Silence.

Coming.
You are near.
You are close.
You are here.

Run

AMY CAMPBELL

I CAN FEEL THE BLOOD PUMPING in my veins, feel my heart struggling to keep up a rhythm, feel that strange rush of adrenaline that kicks in just when you know that you physically cannot run anymore. I stumble on, trying to keep at the incredibly difficult, yet necessary pace I have set for myself. I chance a look back, and breathe out a ragged sigh of relief. My pursuer is nowhere to be seen. I have lost him. For now.

I run to the beat of my feet pounding against the ground, like music only I can hear. The rhythm keeps me going, and I keep running. Where I'm going, I'm not exactly sure. Just so long as it's somewhere that he can't find me. I dodge in and out of the trees, and hop over roots and fallen branches on the ground. The woods have always been an intimidating place, with big trees that block out the sunlight and strange sounds. It's even more frightening when you are being chased.

I feel my breath catch in my throat and my chest begins to protest. I do some quick math in my head. At this rate, I should only be able to keep going for about three more minutes before I collapse. I'll keep running for now. I count the number of times my feet hit the ground to keep my mind occupied. It's better than thinking about how tired I am, how dark it is, or how close he is. I figure out the average number of times my feet hit the ground in ten seconds. And, despite the seriousness of the situation, a smile breaks out across my face.

Math has always been something I can rely on. It has been my safety blanket. About a month ago, a man started following me. He left messages on my phone in the middle of the night. He was always behind me, although I never saw his face. He left notes around my house. He would whisper my name and wake me up. And now he was chasing me. I recited the seven times tables in my head to calm myself. The last month I have been on edge, always looking over my shoulder. Everything disappeared around me, things I thought I could count on were suddenly nowhere to be found. But numbers don't change. One plus one will always be two, whether or not there's a man chasing you.

By my calculations, I should only have a few seconds left. I find one last bit of energy to push myself forward, to give myself that last rush of movement, and then it is over. I collapse onto the ground. It is cold, and uncomfortable and rough. I breathe in, trying to soothe my aching lungs. I lie there for some time, just counting. And then I hear the footsteps again.

It is him, he is here. They get louder, he is catching up. I need to get up, run away. But I have lost the ability to move. My legs are no longer controlled by me, and no matter how much I will myself to move I am still trapped. The footsteps get louder and louder, he is coming to get me. I fight the urge to scream. And then, I can hear him breathe, so loudly that I know he must be only inches away. I can sense him next to me, feel his glare. I force my eyes open and take a frantic look around.

I see only trees.

⌒

I wake up shaking, and look around me. Everything is white. White walls, white floors, white lilies, white hospital bed. The man. Running. Counting. Falling. People. Doctors. Being sent here. The lock on my door. The drugs they pump into me every day until I can't even remember my own name, never mind what exactly happened. I still don't quite understand. I get flashbacks, like I am watching a slideshow. It doesn't seem like these are my memories; it is as though I am watching someone else's life.

All I know now is the things the doctors tell me. There never was a man. Aside from that, nothing is certain anymore. I can't remember my name, age, address, phone number. I don't remember a time before this, a better time. And if you ask me what one plus one is, I won't be able to tell you.

⌒

The Clichés Are Ready and Waiting

Hannah O'Boyle

You are a flirt, I'm sure
and I am misunderstood.
If this wasn't real life
we would make the perfect movie.
But since this is,
I'm sure we are destined
to fail beautifully.

Needles and Knives

Caelen Feller

The knives licked her skin, a laced cloak of flame,
Criss-crossing, weaving lines of red,
Interspersed by the deep pricks of the needle,
Her face was unrecognisable to me.

I picked her up from the bed of needles,
Still dripping with the serum of her overdose,
But despite the bag that covered her eyes,
The petals unfurled. It began again.

The rose continued to grow.

Entropy

Orla McGovern

I shouldn't have said that.

It probably came across very preachy. I should avoid condescension.

I'm terrible at talking to people. It never goes right.

Why do I hate it? I don't hate it. I just need the excuse. I want the upset, the self-loathing.

Why do I doubt my motives? I should stop questioning my thoughts.

Why do questions scare me?

What am I scared of?

Why am I asking questions?

Don't I know already?

If I know, why can't I admit it?

I wish I could stop.

Why do I want to stop?

I want to stop thinking.

Why can't I stop thinking?

What is wrong with me?

Please stop thinking.

Stop thinking.

Please.

Stop.

To Find a Name

Caelen Feller

THE KNIFE IN HER HAND is cold, but only just. She walks out into the hazy twilight, whispering her name for reassurance. 'Linda, Linda, Linda ... Linda?' Thinking for a while, she comes to the conclusion that this name is simply not suitable anymore. She will have to acquire a new one, as soon as possible. Simply making up a name won't do though, a name must be taken. But where to find one?

As she grips the handlebars of her bike, Linda's arms shake, almost imperceptibly. The guttural growl of the bike's engine shatters the heavy silence that lies in the air. A bat drops from the trees above. It lands in front of the bike, startling her. She regains her composure quickly, realising there is no danger from the small creature. Linda likes bats. She had one as a pet once, but she can't remember what happened to it in the end. The bat's name was Jenny, maybe? No, something else ... Vera? Yes, that sounds right.

'I'm going to call you Vera,' she whispers to the bat. The bat does not understand this, unsurprisingly, but as it is much too dazed to fly away, Vera goes with Linda.

Linda used to read books, before. She still has some in her room. As she goes to the shelf, she feels a strange tingling at the back of her mind, as if she has forgotten something. However, she ignores this. Sitting, she picks a book from the shelf and begins to read to Vera. Her voice is hoarse, and she struggles with the words. Linda enjoys reading, but does not often get the chance. As she reads, she remembers, but not very much. She reads on, until sleep takes her.

When Linda wakes, something is obscuring her vision. Standing, she pries the sleeping bat from her face. In the far corner of the room is a dollhouse. She removes the mutilated furniture from the house and gingerly puts Vera inside. She then walks away, humming. As she walks, things begin to slip from her mind. Things about bats, about stories and the memories they brought, good ones, memories she would like to keep. She may lose these memories, but they will never leave her, not really.

The business of taking a name is a tricky one, and Linda isn't entirely certain how she will go about it. She knows it will first be necessary for her to travel a while. From there, she will know what to do. She has faith in herself, even if she is not sure why. She walks to her bike, and begins the journey. She is not worried about losing her way. It will be a long journey, and will take time. As she rides, Linda watches the sunrise. She thinks only of the road in front of her.

It is sunset by the time Linda reaches the house. It feels right to her, feels of beginnings. It stirs many memories, ones she would rather not remember. The doors to the house are secured with heavy chains. She remembers the bolt cutters though, in the outhouse. She left them there, after she finished. After rummaging in the dark for some time, she finds them, and opens the doors. Without the support of the chains, the doors collapse, their hinges unable to support them. She waits for a moment, until the dust settles. She makes an effort to clear the entryway of debris, but it is tedious work, work she dislikes. The darkness of the house is comforting, it welcomes her.

What is inside is of no surprise to Linda. As she picks her way through the dried bodies of the bats, she feels like she is forgetting something. The bats are only partially there. They all seem to have chunks missing from them. Most rooms of the house are empty of life. However, Linda stays well clear of the extremities of the house, the cellar and the attic. She knows that these parts of a house are never empty.

She leaves the house with a single item. As she leaves, she takes care not to make too much noise – she knows her searching could have attracted unwanted attention. Linda's hands tremble as she stands on the steps, a scrap of paper clutched in her hand. She doesn't want to remember the things that happened here, what she did. As she forces the memories away, her trembling hands become peaceful again.

Linda has found what she came for. She has no cause to stay any longer. The woods surrounding the house and road are not welcoming to her. They carry with them a certain wish to be left alone. Though some urge causes Linda to think of this place in the woods as home, she knows it is not, and can never be. It holds nothing for her anymore, and it is not her home.

As she lights a match and watches the house burn, she sees a bat fly from the smoke. She thinks of Vera and longs for company. But she soon forgets, staring blankly into the flames. She forgets everything, forgets Linda.

Throwing the paper into the flames, she walks away.

Those Temptations

Emma Shevlin

There's an open bottle,
Bubbles breaking free.
The smell is quite enticing,
It's got a grip on me.

But I won't take a sip.
The drug won't quench my thirst.
Even though my head and heart
Are nearly fit to burst.

There's an open fag box
With cylinders to light,
To blow away my problems.
I could give up the fight.

But I won't take them out.
The tips will not glow red.
My teeth will not go yellow.
The smoke won't fill my head.

There's a knife right here,
A blade that has been sharpened
Ready to carve into my skin;
The flesh that can be opened.

But I won't pick it up.
It won't change a thing.
Cuts just leave some ugly scars
With a momentary sting.

These methods of forgetting
Will quickly fade away.
I widen my eyes and look around;
There's a bigger game to play.

A Frozen Life

SAMUEL H. DOYLE

There lies the suckling babe at mother's breast,
A slight inconsequential life, defenceless.
How are you now?
Infant weak and powerless, transformed and yet
Ravaged by the incessant revolutions of time.
A haughty figure, condescending, has stolen your place.
A babe no more but an indeferential heartless creature,
Mutated by lusty power and subsequent
Ignorance of your abuses.
This life shamed with the prolonged suffering
And terrible injustice of old age.

For now you do attempt futilely to depart
From your enveloping and everlasting sorrows,
For you feel your last winter come upon you.
The snow falls thick; an indomitable blanket of white,
Encroaching, invading, seizing, suffocating.
Out of the favoured haunt of despots and brigands
You emerge resplendent in an ale-encouraged sheen of sweat,
Rags reeking with that distinguished alcoholic aura,
The proclaiming stench of your hob-nailed path to eternal
damnation.

A body drunk meanders through the building drifts,
More likened to ash they seem in your confusion.
Your stressed inebriated mind echoes eerily

In sodden slush-filled wanderings.
A tempered stride leading from the fore,
Its hopeless aim the well-trodden path of life;
That elusive route always escaping you.
Your ramblings begin to weave off course, a weary trudge
As you waken from your liquor-induced stupor.
For now you see the damning life you chose.

Your end is fast approaching.

Your weighted step does falter, uncertain
As you succumb to an unmitigating fear.
Now you know the truth, poor man.
One frail stumble of that broken soul,
Bent from the killing dust of coal man's lungs,
Shielding scraps torn asunder by the icy
Death-ringing winds of frozen lives and winter storms.

You have reached your final fall.
Ceasing, blue to the skin, you force
Frostbitten seized-up limbs into a ball of frost.
A poor excuse this hollow makes
For your final resting place.
Curled tight, as your life blood freezes
To the ice from which your heart is derived.

You lie, a freezing beggar, at Mother Nature's breast,
One slight inconsequential life, defenceless.

She Said

GRACE COLLINS

SHE SAID SHE WOULD RUN away with me. I told her my plans and she sent me directions from the train station to her house along with twenty euro for a ticket. She said that once we got there we would go to the docks and ask one of the cargo ships if they would take us. We would tell them that we would cause no trouble; we would get off at the first stop because once you're on the continent you are able to travel easily. They would agree and we would give them fake names and tell them that we were lovers and that we were fleeing from our families who didn't approve of our affair. At night she would play with my hair as I sang until the two of us were fast asleep.

And when we arrived at the first port we would thank the kind men and get off. And we'd busk on the streets until we had enough money to get a train to the furthest place that we could get to. We would take it all in. Watch the world that we've known for so long slip away as new hills and winding rivers replaced them. And we'd ride until we got kicked off. And we would never have a problem with passing over borders because we could charm our way out of anything.

And we'd reach a town where we'd meet a nice man who was driving to the city in the morning. And he would take us in for the night and we would stay with his family and play games with his dog and in the morning he would take us in his car to the city so we could try and get jobs. And we'd waitress in a dingy diner for a few weeks. Singing to the cooks and dancing with the brooms. All this before leaving again. We would never stop. We would get by on what we had; two small suitcases and barely enough money to make our next trip, pay cheque to pay cheque. We wouldn't read the papers, or listen to the news; none of it matters.

We would never stay more than a month in one place. There is so much to see. Isn't this the best way to see it? She would never make me feel guilty and I would never remind her of what we had left behind. We would be happy happy and if we didn't like somewhere, we would leave. Simple as that. Two girls with nothing to hold them back.

Forever and always faithful to each other.

Damp Tissues

ORLA McGOVERN

Why do you cry?
You believe in
Life eternal.

Your family's
In heaven, right?
Just gone to God.

Surely that death
Is better than
This painful life.

Why grief and black
Not the joy and
White of new life?

Painting in the Dark

Samuel H. Doyle

I SOON REALISED I COULDN'T get it, what everyone else got: that exhilarating feeling as you pulled the trigger, the rush of testosterone as I snatched the cash. I felt like a hollow shell in comparison; I needed more, much more. So I began my own little journey of discovery.

It was a dark night, if I remember well, for the moon was a tiny silver crescent concealed for the most part by dull clouds. It felt rather lonely outside in the shadowy alleyway, with a lone streetlamp for company, wreathed in the sticky smoke of the factory suburbs. As I stood there, stooping in the bar doorway, this woman went wandering by. She appeared to know she was in the wrong part of town; she was leaning forward clutching her arms to herself and darting her head behind her at regular intervals.

I knew right then what could make me tick. I rose stealthily, in my mind like a panther creeping from hiding. Using the blackness of the night and the thickness of the smog I followed the lost little creature. Despite the gloom she stood out, the blonde tresses on her head assisting me like a lighthouse guides a trawler home to harbour. A short while later she turned, lengthening her stride, increasing her pace, as she grew confident of safety. Such rashness was her downfall. Literally. She sped up on cobblestones and her heels snapped clean off, throwing her roughly to the uneven ground. All hesitation vanquished, I pounced. One sharp blow to the base of her neck and next my sweating palms were sealing her struggling screams.

A tearing sensation and lots of pain, by God I'd swear that I would have blacked out, defenceless, if not for sheer bloody minded determination and adrenaline bursting through my veins. The desperate vixen had sunk her perfect teeth deep into my finger and was ripping at it viciously. Any pretence at patience or care was thrown by the wayside as I beat her into submission. I could feel her flesh blooming into bruises as my scarred fists flew at her; the sensation was not altogether unpleasant, almost like the texture of slightly squished strawberries, very soft and pliable yet with a mushiness that suggested rot.

I lost all sensations momentarily; almost felt like I was hovering in the sulphuric sky, watching myself dispassionately as I enforced my will. Long after any resistance ceased I leaned back. Only one thought continued to reverberate in my head: 'My arms are bloody tired!' I really felt terrible; apparently no amount of time in the gym was going to make the physical effort of such assaults any easier. I turned back to the innate specimen sprawled bloodily on the cracked curbstones.

There was something decidedly artistic about her pose. I imagined myself as a film director, the new Spielberg, with the power to turn such beauty into a mashed up mucky mess with a few lines. As I dreamed of the possibility I realised that my methods, brutal and barbaric, though requiring extra work, gave satisfaction of heights unattainable by less active, legal means.

To my ultimate surprise a faint moan wafted, like the whistling of an early autumn breeze, upwards to a height where it became barely detectable. An unexplainable rage took hold of me, my guts and organs boiled in anger, visible steam must have poured forth from my orifices as I worked myself up into an unstoppable murderous frenzy. How dare that beaten weakling cling on to the life which I had worked so hard to take away from her, the selfish bitch!

I paused briefly to flex my bulging muscles, bursting with sheer violent emotion, and contorting my hunched back painfully to relieve the aching tension. Then I lunged at the vaguely writhing body, grasping hold of it and heaving it above my head to break her spine in one bone-crunching movement. I could have laughed as I thought of how such an action was more natural and even easier to me than straining my bony fingers to snap a tiny pencil in half. The similar sound of her cracking bone and the pencil lead breaking was captivating.

Still feeling cheated by her earlier refusal to die, I decided to ensure that there could be no possible repeat of offensive survival. Almost snakelike, I sinuously slid a combat knife from my tough hide boots and slowly slit her dainty perfumed throat. The sight awaiting me awoke feelings and emotions never before discovered. I found pure joy in this visage of incomparable beauty. A new gleaming smile of my creation gazed up at me, luscious poppy red lips pulsing ever so slowly, coating the grin with an ever thicker layer of sticky, shiny gloss. It brought my mind back to the lazy spurting of the chocolate fountain I got for Christmas last year.

I stayed with this heavenly apparition until near dawn, stricken by a love that has not yet found an equal, a passion deep, thirst unquenchable, desire insatiable that forever guides my life to following this night time pastime. As the sun rose blearily around the towering chimneystacks I walked away, glancing back only once to see the pale torso and jeans, freshly dyed and clotted brown, lying in a drying puddle.

The masterpiece of a very special abstract artist.

Or Don't

CAELEN FELLER

Lie in the snow.

It may chill you, but you won't freeze.

Climb the hill; the house's gaping windows stare at you, ever watching.

You may feel the urge to enter.

Listen to your instincts and open the doors.

Don't be afraid of the dark.

Search the house, and find the object that reminds you most of home.

Take it.

Visit the outhouse; you will find a shovel.

Don't touch the rake – it has blood on the handle.

Dig a hole in the hard, frozen ground.

Bury the object.

Find something else.

Take it.

Find a home that matches.

The Shadows

HANNAH-ROSE MANNING

I have always feared the shadows.
Raven-black in colour, shifty in shape.
My teddy said the shadows were dangerous.
'They'll draw you in and keep you there.'

In daytime they whispered softly to me.
'Come to us, Sarah, come.'
No choice but to follow.

Noon. They shrink. I grow,
No longer afraid.
But they creep back,
Lengthening fear.

When the clock struck nine,
The night stole them away.
Daytime vampires.

Morning. They're back.
With their sinister smiles.
Grown-ups say, 'Shadows can't hurt you.'
But Teddy and I know best.

Beautiful Gas Mask

CONOR KELLEHER

YOUR NECK.

Bare, because of the heat. Working my way down, there's the standard patchy haz-mat kit that everyone wears. You wear it well. Even lower, the legs, deep scratches in the thick material. Lower still, the boots, scuffed and worn from a probable lifetime of hiking. If we go up, there's the back of your head, your short brown hair and the strap of your gas mask.

It's so horrifically incomplete.

That's all that's left. All I have to remember you by. The last I saw before the earth noticed us and swallowed you whole.

It isn't enough. It won't ever be.

I sit down on a nearby rock, just feet from where the ground caved in. Everything is the same black, stodgy colour through the tint of the gas. The sky is black, the ground is black, the nearby ocean is black, the horizon is black, and the hole you disappeared down is black. The haze hangs low over everything, clutching the earth like a blanket smothering a baby.

We had been walking. Making our pilgrimage.

We'd done it, where no one else had. We'd gotten through the forests, where the trees would kill you just to watch you bleed, we made it through the barren deserts that were more toxin than sand, and we'd made it through the metropolis full of the hopeless who never knew to wear a gas mask all those years ago when all this began. We'd done it. We'd survived. We were a few hours from our destination, at most. Maybe even less.

And then the ground ate you.

～

My eyes are stinging in that strange way they do when the mask is leaking. I panic, startle, fumble with the systems check, but no, everything is safe and secure. Or so the readings say. They've never lied before.

It's gone. That snapshot of your back. The last I had of you. No, not gone. Slipping. I let it slip. It isn't worth anything. Let it slip. Let you slip. For the best. I've got a job to do, and thinking about you isn't going to help anything. It's best if I just forget. Forgetting's always easy. I don't have time for this. I don't have time for you.

I stand up.

And I sit back down.

And then I lie down.

And then I remember.

Remember pulling you from the roots that held you. Remember you pulling me from the acrid acid sludge as it bore down to swallow me. Remember the way one of the hopeless had held on to you and how angry that had made me, deep inside, how I knew I had to make you safe, how I crushed his head against the wall and caved in his skull and it was like he didn't notice but I didn't notice either because I was too busy noticing you.

You were the one thing that wasn't poison.

And maybe you were, a little. But it was the good kind of poison. The one that takes you softly, and quietly. Gently. We could use a lot more of that, around here.

⌒

The eyes have stopped stinging. Now they're glazing over with wet, as if to blind me from the present and force me to remain in the past. Fine by me. I'm here. Our goal is just a short way away, now. I could stay here for hours, days, years, if I wanted to, remembering you.

Words come into my mind. Words from before everything went wrong. They haven't fit anything here, anything in this place, for a long, long time. But they fit you.

If I close my eyes and still my breathing, I can almost feel you lying beside me.

Almost.

I reach out an arm to touch you. You're there and not there at the same time. I hold you as best as I can. But you're slipping. Everything's so hard to remember. Your hand, both in mine and not, my arms, both around you and not, your laugh, shaky and distorted by the Com you spoke through, ringing loudly in my mind but silently everywhere else.

I wish the ground hadn't eaten you. I wish it a lot.

I've never wished for anything before.

I try to remember why we did this, why we came here in the first place. It was important, the reason. We talked about it. Neither of us could remember. That happens here; memories die, new ones come in to replace them. We tried to eke out our story as we went along. We'd come from a safe place, a happy place, maybe, and we'd been chosen to go out and do this. To reach it. Whatever it was.

I can't remember and I don't much care. The kind of safe and happy that place made me feel pales in comparison to the kind you could provide. I'm angry. Not at anything in particular. But I'm angry that you died. I want you back. It isn't fair, and it isn't right, and I'm not going to press on because I want you back right now, right now, and if the ground doesn't produce you and give you back to me then I don't know how I'll do it but I'll burn this entire planet even worse than it already is, and it will think back to the cancer ravaging it now with fondness and it will wish it had given me everything I ever wanted because as much as I'm rending and coming undone and splitting apart at the seams it's nothing compared to the damage I want to wreak on this worthless excuse for a patch of ground to stand on.

I'll do it.

I will.

I'll kill everything.

Maybe that's how things got like this in the first place.

I don't know.

Neither do you.

We can't remember.

No one can remember.

I'm lost and I don't know where I've been and I don't know where I'm going and I can't remember who I am and I don't even have you anymore and soon I'm going to forget you.

◦

I jerk awake.

No. No, no, no, no, no. No.

But yes.

It's what happens, what always happens, the memories will leave and die and then I'll be alone and I'll never know I was ever anything different.

And then I start screaming. And my memory may be working with a skeleton crew, but I know I've never screamed like this before. It's rage and fear and anger and pain and everything and all of me, all wrapped up in one fatal gesture, and I turn on the Com as far as the dial will go and everyone, everywhere, for miles around will know this sound and they'll know I was here and they'll know how I felt and then, and then,

Then they'll forget.

～

And I want to make some sweeping gesture, some wonderful speech, a pledge to never forget and to always remember, but no matter what reminders I make for myself, no matter how many times I carve your name onto my skin, the reality is that the memory will die and then I'll be alone again.

Can I even remember your name?

No. I can't.

I chase the memory all around my head. I can't quite manage to catch it.

And then my thoughts are quiet for the first time in a long while and I hear the ocean bubbling two miles away and I hear the wind rustle over this bleak rocky wasteland and I hear the gas shifting in the air and I hear the far-away scuttling of whatever lives here and, I have to say, to me at least, it all sounds pretty much the same as silence.

And then I see light, cutting through the gas like a knife.

Emanating from the hole you fell into.

And I'm only thinking one thing: That light's artificial.

No. Sorry. Two things.

That light's artificial,

And that light's *you*.

No. Not yet. I can't have you come back and then be torn away like this. I can't believe it yet.

I won't.

It'll hurt too much.

I run to the edge, and I stare down the depths. The beam of

light cuts my eyes but does little to disrupt the black shroud below, underground. The light begins to flicker, on and off, and something registers in my brain, dots and dashes and pieces of a code I can't name, much less use.

Your Com is broken. Must be. This is you communicating. That would make sense.

It's also impossible. You're dead.

Dead. Dead dead dead dead dead and not coming back. I'm not doing this. I'm not hurting myself like this. I refuse.

Coms.

I have spares.

It's like someone loaded a shotgun full of buckshot and let it off inside of me. I feel so happy, it's like my organs are rupturing. I didn't know relief could feel this cancerous. This isn't real, it isn't, and all the happiness I let it have in me will sour and rot and I'll feel all the worse for ever having let it in and just be *quiet*.

I whisper into my Com: 'If you can hear me, turn the light off.'

Abruptly, the beam cuts.

'Throw it back on.'

The light beams back into existence.

And there it is, there you are, there's the proof, there's the miracle, there's the sign that you're fine, there's all the things that I didn't let myself want, there's you and there's you and there's you and there's you and there's you.

Alive. Lung-breathing, heart-beating, blood-boiling, mind-whirring, jaw-clenching, back-arching, eyes-smiling, properly, truly, alive.

There are no words. There will never be enough words to express any of what I need expressed.

But I don't care.

You're alive.

⌒

'*You*,' I choke. Choking. Gas mask must be leaking. Don't care. You're alive.

'I'm throwing you a Com,' I whisper, voice oddly broken. I take the small black thing from my pack and drop it as gently as I can. I don't hear it hit the bottom.

A voice flickers from inside my mask. 'Can you hear me?'

And I am a child, staring wide-eyed at the sun. '*You.*'

'Me,' you agree.

This is too much. This is much too much. This isn't what's happening. I'm on the rock. My mind is broken. I tossed the mask off in despair and these are the hallucinations that come as I am poisoned to death. It would explain why I'm shaking so much. This isn't allowed. Nothing this beautiful would ever be allowed to happen down here. Not ever.

'Really?'

'I'm here. I heard you screaming. Are you okay?'

I try to tell you that I'm fine, but I'm shaking, like the tops of those mounds where the poison in the earth's veins would burst out. We saw plenty of them earlier on, on the plains. You always got advanced warning, they were shaking so much, and then gas would radiate outwards. The gas concentration was far too high to be filtered.

Neither of us could remember how we knew that.

But, those mounds.

That's me.

You're the poison.

I don't know what the explosion will look like.

~

'Are you okay? Why were you screaming?'

You're concerned, I know, but there isn't, I can't, I couldn't begin …

'*You,*' I manage.

Barely.

And I don't know what to do or what to say or how I feel, because you don't let anyone mean anything to you down here, because it all gets taken away, and it's not worth it, and I know that, I do, but, I just, *you.*

'Where are you?' I ask, trying to shake the thoughts out of my head, like releasing bad fumes from the mask when they build up.

'Underground. A tunnel caved in. I can follow it.'

'Or I could follow you.'

'You'd die. I fell with the cave floor. The harsh rocks and

splintering rafters broke my fall.'

I smile. You're joking. You're not making sense, so you're joking. 'That's not how falling works.'

'My leg is broken.'

'What?'

'My leg. I can still go on. I'll follow this tunnel, give you directions, you follow me above. These are old mining tunnels, I can tell from the wooden supports. They'll reach the surface somewhere. We'll just keep on walking.'

Not joking. 'Your leg? Broken? Can the medi–'

'Irreparable. It doesn't matter. We're already at the end. It'll be fine. I'm starting.'

The light dies out. You're putting it to work underground, now.

'Start walking forwards. I'll tell you when to turn. Can you do that?'

I can, and I do.

⁓

There's relief, and concern, and confusion, and a bundle of other emotions our language hasn't been kind enough to name, all bubbling inside of me and I don't know what the end result is supposed to look like. So I think about that for a time.

And then I do something else:

'Your leg. Does it hurt?'

Another silence. Not so long. 'Of course it does.'

Of course it does. How could it not?

But something's wrong.

'Isn't it … bad?'

I don't have words. I'm sorry.

'I'm not going to let it slow me down. I can forget it. I can keep on walking.'

I know you can. That wasn't what I was trying to say. 'I don't want you to forget.'

What was I trying to do? I was just talking. What do these words even mean? Pain is everywhere, all the time; it's a necessary part of life. Why should it be any different? Give pain too much power, it'll slow you down. I know that. We remember it from somewhere, both of us do. I appreciate that you don't say it.

'Never mind. I shouldn't have said anything. It's nothing important.'

'We need to turn left now.'

We do.

'What you think is important, you know. I want to hear it.'

I have a lot to say and no way to say it all, but you're here, and you're listening, and that's as good as it gets. 'You don't have to forget. We forget so much. If you hadn't survived the fall ...'

I don't know what I'm trying to say. But I think, somehow, you do.

'Pain is different. It's not useful. It's better to forget.'

'It's not about what's useful. It's about what's important.'

'Living is more important right now. We need to keep on walking.'

There's a silence. Not a bad one. Comfortable. Room to breathe. A quiet, comfortable cave to sleep in, rather than a dead, barren, barely-survivable desert.

There's the wind. There's the sea. There's the scuttling. There's the shifting of the gas. And there's the oddest hissing noise, too, seemingly coming from my mic. Again, the readings say I'm fine, and if the readings are wrong, then there's no point in worrying. It's too late by then.

In the distance, there are shadows moving on the hills. Big, fearsome things, things that dive for the weak and devour the defenceless. We aren't worried. We are not strong, and we are not defended, but they're at the hills.

We keep on walking.

⌁

We're walking, but not together. Talking, being with one another, but apart. Our hands are held, but not. The air rustling through my open fingers is ruining the illusion. I need you again soon.

We walk past a hill and suddenly the sea is behind it, and the tunnel is leading to a small island. It's not on the way to where we need to be, but we've got time, and no other real choice, so we walk along the narrowing path to where we're sure the old mining tunnels would have been.

This bridge is no more than fifteen metres across at its widest, and it's made of jagged rock; sharp, brittle shale that's tough to walk on. We're not walking overly quickly, so I break a few pieces off and toss it into the sea. The second it's out of my hand it's black rock over black sludge through black gas, and it may as well be invisible. The sea swells.

'Were there other people with us, before?'

You don't break the silence forcefully, but I still jump when you do. 'Sorry?'

'Did we set off with just the two of us, or were there others?'

I shrug. Then, realising you can't see, I say: 'I'm not sure. I don't remember.'

'Me neither, but that isn't exactly worth much.'

'No. Not really.'

A stupid question eats at my head. I try to drown it, but I remember what you said earlier, about being important. 'Why do you ask?'

And the second I say it I know for sure it's stupid and worthless and that you think less of me, but before I can do anything self-destructive about it, you talk: 'Your scream, earlier—'

A pause. A long one. You never pause.

Something's wrong.

'What is it?' I bark.

'Something big, and scuttling, and —'

Your voice is getting fainter. You're running to the tunnel's exit. I follow.

And as I do, I notice something.

The ocean doesn't roll, and the waves don't break, not like our language and the metaphors we end up using seem to imply that they once did. The ocean is toxic and acid and unstable and bubbling. But not now. Something's in it. Stirring.

And then, like a mole sticking its head above the surface of the earth, there's a shiny black carapace in the waves.

And then another.

And another.

And then they constitute an ocean all of their own.

Big things, fearsome things, things that thrive on weakness and fear and pain.

Why here? Why now?
I turn to look at the mainland.
Oh.

⮑

I can't remember what a dawn looks like. No one can. But I know what it's supposed to look like. The sun, a great ball of fire, would creep over the horizon, and all its light would spill over the hills and bathe the green countryside in amber and red and everything would be alright and the forces of evil would scream, scatter, steam, melt, and the heroes would rejoice and it would be *glorious*.

Well, this is like that. Except, instead of the sun, there's black, and instead of the green countryside, there's black, and instead of amber and red rolling into view there's black. Like the hands of an angry god, reaching for me, the ant it could never crush, the disease it could never purge, the stain it could never remove, and I can see its face in this hellish sunset and I can see it smile in triumph.

I am not in awe. There is never a time for that here. Awe is just waiting for death.

I turn on my heels and run.

You've already left. The things wouldn't let you wait.

I keep running.

It's a rock. It's a high, steep rock, in the middle of the ocean, with a thin shale bridge. That's what we're on. And all around us is a sea of toxic sludge, or a sea of sleek, strong, hungry things. It doesn't look good. It looks like death.

I think about what brought them here. What could have been loud enough, alluring enough, to attract this amount of these things? Whatever it was, it must have sounded horrifically wounded. Easy pickings.

I don't curse my luck. I don't care enough to. The worst that can happen is I die.

Not quite.

The worst that can happen is that *you* die.

⮑

And then I'm off the bridge entirely and I'm shouting in my Com for you and I don't see you or hear you and there isn't any exit in sight and then there it is, just a hole in the ground and you run out and you twist and then there's that thing in your arms, I remember, from so long ago, that long, thick, heavy metal thing, I can't remember what it does.

And then there's a flash of red and the hole is collapsing in on itself and I remember.

And then I'm running to you.

And then I'm screaming for you.

And then you turn to see me.

And then I've run to you.

And then I'm staring at you.

And your gas mask is staring back.

I want –

I want a lot of things. And all of them are you.

⌒

But there aren't words for this, there aren't actions, there isn't any way to convey and if there ever has been I can't remember and you get one chance to make your gesture down here, and I want to make mine count, but I don't even know how to begin.

'*You*,' I start.

You shake your head. 'No. *You*.'

And then there's death behind us and we're running, and you're limping and you're turning and slowing and I grab your hand to pull you along but you're just aiming and then there's red and the things scream as they die and you throw your weapon away and I'm guessing it's either empty or you know that we can't fend off this many and then we come to the edge of the island, the edge of the rock, the end of the rope and the end of the line and the end of the end of the end.

We stop.

And we look down.

And there are rocks below that would kill us before we could dissolve in the sludge. A painless death, that. As painless as they come, anyway.

I look at you.

I don't want to die.

I don't want you to die.

But – 'Looks like this is it.'

You nod. You're staring at what's coming. I can almost see your face through the visor of your gas mask. I've never tried before, but if I focus, I can almost see your –

I look away. 'We were so close.'

'Close to what? Why can't this be it? Why can't this be where we were headed?'

'This?' I shake my head. 'How can *this* be it?'

'Neither of us can remember, anyway. It may as well be here. This is as good a place to end up as any.'

A pause, before you continue.

'You do realise why they're here?'

I don't.

'Your scream.'

And it makes sense.

And it hurts.

It does.

Screams never go unanswered here.

◦

But before I can say anything: 'No, don't be sorry. I'm glad. It made me remember.'

I'm still holding your hand, from before.

I'm not going to stop.

'Do you remember my name?' I ask you.

You shake your head.

'I don't remember yours, either. It doesn't matter. Names aren't important.'

And I close my eyes. And I breathe. This. This is important. This matters. This, right here, is the moment where everything falls into place. This is where everything becomes defined. If someone picks up my gas mask in the distant future, long after my body has rotted away, and they wonder, briefly, who I used to be, then I want this to be the answer.

'*You.*'

Your hand squeezes mine in thanks.

And then –

'I could take the mask off, if you like. Do you want to see my face?'

I know what you're saying, and I know what you're saying it for. The gas doesn't matter anymore, so neither does the mask. This is an offer you could only make at the end.

But no.

'I don't need it to need you.' I say. Honestly. 'It's a beautiful gas mask. You should keep it on.'

You nod. I nod.

And here it comes.

Here comes death.

And we turn from whatever's behind us because it doesn't matter anymore. We're facing the writhing sea. And our hands are together. And we are together. And everything we know is behind us and death is all around us but we're standing and we're hand in hand and this is right, this is it, this is how it happens, this is perfect.

Well. Almost perfect.

I grab your hip, and I pull you in. Your arms fit around my neck. And we –

We melt together.

And as we melt –

We drop.

Three Balanced Meals

Hannah O'Boyle

For breakfast I had pills
washed down with sorrow.

Later on, I feasted
on my own self doubt.

I finished off the day
with a cool descent into lunacy.

(I am not starving myself,
I am just feeding my sadness.)

Little World of Faith

Emma Shevlin

THEY'VE STARED AT THIS WINDOW so many times before.
The glint of sunlight switching colours as it shines through each
separate piece of glass. Someone's mother nudging them to get
up for Communion because they are holding other people up,
slowly trudging up and down to receive their little piece of God.
Desperately trying to remember where their seats are.

When you're in this large stone building, you're in your own little
world of faith. No-one notices him sneak in the back. No child there
comments on his odd appearance and twitching eyes, and not one
person notices the gun.

⌐

Off-piste

Hannah-Rose Manning

I USED TO LOVE SKIING. The feel of soft snow gently whipping against my cheeks, the exhilaration of shooting down a mountain at top speed and landing in a dishevelled heap at the bottom. I used to feel invincible, as though nothing could touch me, my problems lifted away like a feather floating in the breeze. Now I know better, now I know the dangers of the woods ...

It was the eighteenth of May, exactly two months ago. My parents were away on one of their 'special and exclusive' trips that they go on every month and fail to include my sister and me in. Every time the door of our house closes against us, I see my sister's bitten lip, useless tears filling her eyes and her whole body shaking as she begs them to return. I'm fifteen, however, almost a grown up. I'm used to these things and I simply shrug my shoulders, not knowing what else I should do. I have no words to comfort her, nothing to excuse my parents for my vulnerable, seven-year-old sister except, 'Let's go skiing. We'll see them soon enough.'

We grabbed our gear and set off. I live in Colorado, the snowy state, where there is not much to do but ski and ski and ski. Luckily for us, there is a ski slope right beside our huge, majestic house. It is always filled with ornaments and grand furniture, but never with people.

The snow was beautiful that morning, soft and smooth, as the first skiers were just beginning to glide on the thick blanket of snow that draped over the ground. My sister headed immediately for the moderately easy slopes, her dark blonde hair billowing in the mountain air and her chubby cheeks sparkling with the cold. I agreed to meet her at the chairlift and went over to my favourite slope, a challenging, steep, bumpy slope that is the best in Colorado. I flew down it, glancing every now and then at the woods that draw me to them every time.

I did not give in, remembering my parents' last words: 'The

woods are dangerous, Maria, more dangerous that you would ever imagine. Sinister things lurk there. You would not be wise to go in, no matter how experienced you think you are. Avalanches and sharp rocks can kill.'

As I mulled over my parents' last words, I felt a sharp burst of anger and defiance spread over me. *Why should I follow their advice? They've never been role models to Melissa and me. They leave us every month – they don't even care what we get up to as long as we 'don't go into the woods'. And what, may I ask, is so wrong with the woods? They're magical and enthralling and my skiing is of expert level.*

I've skied every boring little mountain in Colorado, why can't I ski this one? 'Because,' a tiny little voice chimed in my head. 'You don't know what dangers lurk there.' I angrily brushed the voice away. I was going in the woods and no one was going to stop me – not Mum, or Dad, not Melissa and certainly not myself!

I stepped gingerly off the slope and slipped into the woods. I stared around in awe. There was sparkling snow dripping from the evergreen trees and the trees themselves were broad and welcoming. A tiny chestnut rabbit hopped a few feet away from me and I shouted with joy as I began to ski. Slow at first, but gradually getting faster and more confident as I whipped through the woods, singing to myself. I had never felt so alive, so perfectly happy. Little did I know it was all about to change.

I stopped abruptly, slipping off my skis. I could feel the presence of another being in the woods. A cold chill ran down my quivering spine as a dark figure came into my sight. I stepped back with shock. He was tall, very tall, and gangly. His face was pale and pinched and his eyes sparkled bright red. His lips, blue with cold, were twisted into what I interpreted as a cruel smile. He seemed unnatural, not of this world. Yet I was transfixed by him.

'Hello, Maria,' he leered. 'What are you doing here? Have you come to play with Danger?'

I don't know how, but I plucked up the courage to speak. 'The w-woods aren't d-dangerous, are they?' I stammered.

He sighed, with obvious annoyance. 'They get more stupid every year,' he muttered. 'No, mundane being. I am Danger, which means you should not cross me by entering my woods. Many have entered and never came back. What makes you think you are so special?'

I evaded his question and asked him, 'Who are you?' He must have heard the obvious wonder and fear dripping from every syllable.

'I am Danger. I am not yet dead but not alive either. I lure foolish skiers into my woods and few ever return. I know what it is like to feel the pull of the woods, the confidence and daring that fills us and chases away all your reason.'

I tried to run but I was frozen to the spot, transfixed by his words. He spoke slowly, a hint of menace in his voice. 'You don't listen, your ears are blocked, and all you hear is false bravado. But I have had my share of trouble. Now, Maria, you must pay for what happened to me. It is your turn. Come with me.'

What I did next was a split-second reaction. If I hadn't, I might have been stuck there forever. All I remember was grabbing my ski and whacking the ghostly spectre with it. He fell to the ground unconscious.

I pulled my skis on and got out of there so fast I could feel the wind whooshing in my ears. I reached the slope and shot a frantic look back in the direction I came from. He was nowhere to be seen. I sighed with relief and realised I was shaking uncontrollably.

Just then, my sister Melissa came skiing up to me. 'I did a blue run,' she said proudly. I smiled weakly and said nothing as she gushed on and on.

The following week, we went skiing once more. I did not go in the woods, nor anywhere near them. I told no one of the phantom keeper of the woods, preferring to keep my encounter secret, although I warned anyone I met not to go in.

They must have had the insight I lacked; I still hear ghostly moans of rage echoing from far away.

I thought wrong

Grace Collins

I WALKED DOWN TO HER apartment block. Three weeks since she'd been there. For three weeks all her stuff had lain untouched by human hands. I had no idea what to expect. I knew they had cleaned the room where she did it; they had to. But would the whole house be like the little princess that I'd nurtured from the day she was born? Or the rebellious teen I'd spent four years arguing with and every day worried if she was going to be okay when she cut us out, and became secretive about her life.

I walked up to the door. Still air met my lips. The apartment was small; pictures lined the hallway. Dancers rinsing out their costumes in St. Petersburg after the show had been a flop but their faces told a different story. They got to dance. A spoiled box of chocolates sweeping away in the wind in Philadelphia the morning after Valentine's Day, left by some rejected lover on the pavement for her to see the beauty in. Herself right when she came home after the hospital. A big smile stretched across her face. It was a genuine smile, the kind that one only has when they really believe in the fact that right now things are going to be okay. They were all taken by her. She never believed in her art, thought she couldn't do it as well as we all saw she could.

It was cleaner then than I remembered her ever saying. Not that she said anything to me. Pretty bottles filled with wilted flowers lined the windowsills. I imagined her collecting them from her friends and rinsing out them in the sink because they held the flowers much better than any vase. An unsent letter sat on the countertop, addressed to that old friend. I wondered if he knew. Should I have delivered that letter with the truth? Or had he read it in the paper?

I left it.

This was too much. I found myself in her room. Handbags organised by both size and colour sat under a large rail full of old sweaters and loose fitting dresses, with baskets of tights and scarves on either end of this makeshift wardrobe. She had been layering up, ready for the cold winter. I sat on her bed. Blankets over blankets met my backside. I counted them; six blankets and a thick duvet to keep out the cold. I ran my hand under the pillow, folded pyjamas just like my little girl had always done. And something else. The box.

I took it out. I shouldn't have done that. The box looked out of place in my hands, in her room, in this apartment but I knew it was hers. I knew because she used to have one in her room as a teenager, I knew it was full of her own little poisons. I cursed myself. I thought I knew what to expect when I came here. I thought she was better. I thought I had done a good job. I'd followed all the books, I'd tried not to push, I had made sure her prescriptions were always filled and that she always took them. I thought, I thought.

I didn't care about my runny nose or the tears on my cheek, I opened the bathroom door. I needed to get out of her room. I surveyed the area, still holding the box. Unlit scented candles lined all available spaces along with mutable beauty products. The scale sat like the monster in the corner. And a small empty bottle of gasoline by the sink. It was a cold room. Too clean, too much for me, this whole place. Why had she done this? Why had she done this!

I crawled into the empty bathtub. This is where she did it. This is what she saw. This. This dingy old place where she lived alone. Here is where they said she lay, here is where she was found. Here is where she poured the liquid over herself, letting it sting her wounds, collect in the hollows of her fragile remains of a body, and here is where she took the flame and let it finally warm her cold soul.

I cried and never returned.

Glitter

SEAN CERONI

I have no mind
And no morals,
Just glitter.

Filling the Void

Caelen Feller

Picture the space between two points,
A and B let's say.
Now think of these points as places,
And the space as far, far away.

Think of these points as vectors,
Moving with mathematical grace.
Think of this distance as growing smaller,
Think of closing the space.

Now think of filling the void,
With words stretching from A to B.
Think of these points as people,
A equal to you, B to me.

First Day

ORLA McGOVERN

Subtle touch of eyes,
Glance, then look away,
An uncertain smile,
Frantic – what to say?

Shift from foot to foot,
Break the old taboo,
Take the leap of faith,
'I'm new ... are you too?'

The Trials of Miss Elisa

Catherine Bowen

I SHOULDN'T HAVE READ that book.

It was too fanciful for me, you knew that when you bought it. I was enraptured by the prose. The long, flowery descriptions drew me in like a light attracts moths and poured ideas into my head until they overflowed and I was forced into action. I couldn't help it. You know how easily influenced I am. If you didn't want me to try to frolic in the woods in a dress, you shouldn't have given me *The Trials of Miss Elisa*. I'm at an impressionable age.

In hindsight, telling you that I was leaving might have been a good idea but I was trying to be whimsical. I knew you would try to crush my new spontaneous attitude or convince me to wear trousers. I crept out while you were watching the rugby. The floorboards creaked horribly with each step but apparently the referee was showing bias so all noise was drowned out by your yells of indignation. I doubted you would even notice my absence.

Fantastic parenting skills, by the way. I'm lucky to have you.

(Why would you watch rugby on one of the five nice summer days we get, anyway? I can admit I felt certain smugness that at least one of us could appreciate the beauty of nature.)

The walk to the woods was lovely. Dappled sunlight streamed through the canopy of leaves created by the trees along the roadside and a cacophony of birdsong joined with the music of the brook to fill the air. (Those lines may come straight from the book but I feel they are appropriate.)

I already felt more graceful, like this walk was filling my eyes with stars and giving me a swan's neck. Maybe I would go wading in the stream or weave wildflowers through my hair. My head was so occupied with these thoughts that I barely registered the blister forming on my toe.

You really should remind me to break in my pumps before using them for walks. Just for future reference.

I pranced onwards, convinced my footsteps were light as the mild summer's breeze that whispered through the trees. (Yes, that was another quote.)

As I reached the laneway that leads down to the forest, I noticed a distinct difference between the novel and reality. While the elegant Miss Elisa danced among the oak trees and flowers, there was never a mention of brambles. The trees in our woods are choked with them. Still, I was determined to be carefree so I held up the end of my dress and stomped down the thorns until I reached the stream. I imagined myself as a dryad, seeking to reclaim her home from the sharp, blackberry-bearing invaders.

I don't think I played the part well. I'm not entirely sure what a dryad is, but I assume they don't curse as much when their ankles are scraped.

Once I reached the stream, I plopped down, not caring about mud or grass stains. I dipped my bleeding ankles into the decidedly not crystal or sparkling waters. It may have been the numbing effect of the freezing water or seeing flowers growing further along the bank but my sense of optimism was revived. In a fit of fancy, I decreed that our calm stream would be forevermore referred to as a babbling brook.

Pleased, I spotted a tall, grand oak tree across the brook. I sprang to my feet with the aim of climbing into it and looking mysterious. I didn't get the chance.

Miss Elisa may be able to wade through her brook with ease but ours has slippery, slimy rocks at its bottom. I toppled and fell as soon as I stood and was utterly drenched in the process.

And to think I could have drowned horribly with no one there to rescue me. Not to mention that I cut my hand on a stone. We're almost out of plasters, just so you know.

After I had stopped shrieking from the cold, I picked myself up out of the stream. (It doesn't deserve to be called a brook.) No birds sang as I hobbled and squelched my way back up to the road. I think I scared them off.

I was despondent. No, that doesn't begin to describe how miserable I was. There's not even a term invented yet. I was dripping onto the road with each step I took and the sun had heated the tarmac enough to stick to my shoe. (One fell off in the brambles and I just couldn't bear the thought of going back for it.) I probably looked like something out of a horror film.

By some great stroke of luck, I had stepped onto the grass and into the shade by the hedgerow when I saw it: Michael O'Shea's car coming down the road. I couldn't risk being seen in that state. I had no choice. Don't you dare tell me you would have done differently in this situation. I did what had to be done.

I dove into the nettles patch.

I have no regrets. This probably saved me from a lifetime of total, soul-crushing mortification. That doesn't mean it didn't hurt though.

So you see, by the time I reached home, I was wet and in pain and miserable. All I wanted was some dock leaves and a bath. But do you know what I got instead? I got to be yelled at, laughed at and finally lectured. I may have 'disappeared with no word of warning' but taking pictures was a cruel and unusual punishment and you know it.

I hope you're happy with yourself.

Irrationality

Samuel H. Doyle

I was afraid of the past
In case it influenced my present

I am terrified of the now
As it will determine my future

I will be scared tomorrow
For I only know fear.

A Walk along the Brussels Road
(An excerpt from a work in progress)

Cahal Sweeney

Introduction

Project pictures/film clips relevant to Napoleonic wars during this speech. Break between each line. Narrator should stand in the middle of stage.

Narrator: Our story begins on the fifteenth of June, 1815. Fourteen months prior to these events, the French emperor Napoleon Bonaparte was captured and sent into exile. He was permitted to bring along 5000 men from his beloved Imperial Guard and rule the tiny island of Elba. He was not to be gone for long however. After eleven months, he returned to France. The newly crowned French king fled and Napoleon was back in full glory.

Horrified, his old enemies met in Vienna to form the Sixth Coalition and plot against one man. The old enemies, listed off the fingers of a hand: Spain, Britain, Prussia, Austria and Russia. Napoleon tried to appeal for peace by appearing publically in white robes as opposed to his famous brown overcoat and sending envoys equipped with treaties to each of the other powers, but any requests for negotiations were overturned. Everyone had learned from their previous mistakes and assumed correctly that Napoleon was not to be trusted. However, despite the danger that faced France, Napoleon's newly reformed army had certain positional advantages. The Austrian and Spanish armies were not mobilised and were encountering logistical problems due to distance. The Russian troops marching all the way from Moscow were not due to arrive for at least a year.

Only two armies, one British under Sir Arthur Wellesley, the Duke of Wellington, the other Prussian under Gebhard Von Blücher, were deployed near France and were in any way prepared for battle. Napoleon had set his sights on Brussels in order to crush both armies simultaneously and establish permanent dominance over mainland Europe. The fate of Europe, and indeed the world, hangs in the balance.

⁓

Act One, Scene One

A tent. Enter Duke of Wellington, his staff, some soldiers etc. Enter Prussian messenger holding a sealed letter

Messenger: Your honour, Arthur Wellesley, Duke of Wellington. I bear news from my leader, marshal of the Prussian Army, Gebhard Von Blücher.

Wellington: What news would this be? I received word of his advance toward Ligny only last night.

Messenger: I bring word of a skirmish, sir. A French army has been sighted in Belgium.

Wellington: *(stunned)* An army!

Messenger: Yes sir. Under the command of the French Emperor himself. Marshal Blücher's 124th Musketeers engaged them. A light skirmish – they seem to have more Voltigeurs than usual – and a brief cavalry charge by French Dragoons. Hardly another Austerlitz but –

Wellington: *(suspiciously)* Did Blücher himself send this message?

Messenger: These words have come from Blücher himself, your Grace. *(Shows him seal on letter)* The armies engaged just as the clock struck eight. I was dispatched at once. Marshal Blücher is going to stand ground at Ligny. This French army, according to spotters, appears to be on a road directly between us. Marshal Blücher feels they want to push us apart, sir.

Wellington: Was there a sighting of Napoleon himself?

Messenger: The Imperial Carriage was spotted at an inn a few miles west of the skirmish, your Grace. Blücher believes that unless this is the biggest bluff the Emperor has ever attempted, he commands them directly.

Wellington: *(nods)* Message received and understood. I must consult with my staff. *(Waves hand behind him)* Send your marshal word that I shall be in touch very soon. You may go.

[Exit Messenger, leaving letter on table]

Wellington: The clock has just struck one. If Napoleon's advance began at seven o'clock, say, they could have advanced a far distance into Belgium. *(Thumps table)* Goddamn it! How could this have happened? Could it be a bluff? Ploys to make us think France is more powerful than they are in reality and hence deter us launching an invasion?

Staff 1: Your Grace, I feel this is no bluff. Why would the Emperor –

Wellington: Silence, Moore.

Staff 2: But sir ...

Wellington: Silence! You all know damn well I don't think this is a bluff, but nor am I willing to accept at present that this blasted French bugger who crept back from exile three months ago would have the nerve to march a full army straight onto British-occupied soil. *(Wellington puts map on table. Staff gather around. Project map of Belgium for audience)*

Staff 3: Assuming that messenger was completely accurate, the Emperor is ...

Staff 2: Your Grace, we do not know for certain that messenger was not a fraud. For all we know, he could be French –

Wellington: With a strong Prussian accent and Blücher's personal seal. No, I do trust him, I believe he is as he says.

Staff 4: Supposing the messenger himself was genuine, do we know for certain that it's the Emperor? Could he not have sent Ney or Grouchy, perhaps?

Wellington: *(Almost amused)* Men, men! I do not wish to believe that it really is Napoleon – I know many of you still think of him as formidable after Spain – but I do not assume he would send Ney or Grouchy to Belgium. It just is not in his character.

Staff 3: Bonaparte sent Ney to conquer Austria –

Wellington: *(Irritated)* While he had taken up residence in an inn twenty miles from the border, yes. However, that was different. *(Bangs table)* Napoleon is a xenophobe who utterly detests the English. Belgium and specifically Brussels is the main centre of British influence on the mainland! Ten years ago, were it not for Nelson, Napoleon would almost certainly have personally led his blasted invasion.

Staff 2: Why would the bugger risk his neck?

Wellington: It was never really war with the coalition. It was always Napoleon against the British. He hates us! He wants nothing more than to beat us off the continent and send any disbanded survivors tearing back to the seven gates of London. He will lead his villainous army in the hope of watching our heroic gin-sodden rags, bless them, blast themselves with their own muskets! He uses scare tactics gentlemen, nothing more! That was what let him conquer half the known world a decade ago but *(raising voice, thumps table with each word)* times … have … CHANGED! Now he must defeat five united empires, along with numerous smaller countries in open warfare. The strategy of Macbeth shall not humble us into submission again.

Staff 1: Your Grace, how would you like us to proceed?

Wellington: Send word to some cavalry skirmishers on the flanks to go hunt for this French army of Blüchers. Find out if it even exists. There's absolutely no point in doing anything else first.

Staff 3: And the gala ball tonight? Shall we send word to Her Grand Duchess of Brussels that His Grace the Noble Duke of Wellington shall not be in attendance?

Wellington: *(Considering)* No. We will proceed with that plan for now. There is absolutely no point in deploying troops or anything else until we know for certain that there is a genuine threat. The Duchess is a rather forceful woman and maintaining good relations with the Belgians is essential for the success of this campaign. And after all *(laughs)* I can't see them attacking in the middle of a celebration. We all know the French dictator fancies his wine as much as assailing us!

In short, pretend that godforsaken army doesn't even exist! Don't let it spoil your evening, my lads!

[Exeunt]

⌒

Act One, Scene Two

A tent. Enter Napoleon and his staff

Napoleon: Has our army congregated as we planned?

Staff 1: Yes, Mon Emperor. Marshal Ney has sent word that he is prepared to take Quatre Bras and later La Belle Alliance. We shall be dining in Brussels by Sunday evening.

Napoleon: Today is Thursday. When shall Ney be ready to strike?

Staff 2: Daybreak, Mon Emperor. The gullible British are unprepared and defenceless. As we speak, their *(sneer)* grand leader, Arthur Wellesley of Wellington, is putting on his finest clothes and dancing shoes for some ridiculous dinner party the Duchess of Brussels is hosting. Their army is spread across the whole country like butter on bread. Ney shall crush them with ease.

Napoleon: Send word to Ney to proceed. I personally wish to speak with Wellington when he is in chains.

Staff 1: I shall see it done, Mon Emperor.

[Exit Staff 1]

Staff 2: And what of the Prussians, sire? What shall be done to deal with their threat?

Napoleon: *(Thinking)* I will engage them personally. Prussians ... annoy me. They are flies to be crushed, specks to be wiped. The British are the true enemies of any Frenchman. However ... Blücher. He is a sly fox. I shall lead the Guard forward. Ney shall capture Quatre Bras. We will destroy both the English and the Prussians at dawn tomorrow and capture Brussels permanently!

Staff 2: As you wish, Mon Emperor.

[Exeunt all but Napoleon]

Napoleon: Oh glorious day! Oh triumphant day! The thought of Wellington in the heart of the Bastille beguiles me. Wellington. The one enemy general who supposedly has the capacity to defeat me in battle. I would have believed it was impossible, a rumour started by a child, but even my own generals do not advise direct contact with him. Were I a Corporal once again, I'd request him to eat grass before breakfast. He and his army are so unfathomably irritating. *(Pacing)* The British. The British Goddamns. I was forced to abandon my campaign in Egypt to deal with traitors in my capital. It was the British who had lashed out against me, spreading their lies and propaganda. It was the British who crippled my fleet at the Nile and finally crushed it at Trafalgar. And the British in the Iberian Campaign ... *(Hollow laugh)* I desired Portugal, a British ally. Spain was no genuine asset, merely a servant to be sent on errands, no more. They had served all their purposes as allies; now they would join the proud league of nationalities under French ascendancy. *(Shout)* But oh no! The traitorous hypocrites chose to join London, not Paris! Pushing my armies north, back over the Pyrenees! But not this time! *(Growling)* Oh, come Ney, take La Belle Alliance, we shall engage the tiresome British on the Brussels road and in our victory, six centuries of shame, insult and pointless conflict will be avenged and the British army will be but a cutlet of meat beneath a French knife!

 [Exit Napoleon]

Act One, Scene Three

A ballroom. Enter Wellington, soldiers, guards, various other nobles/ladies. Music plays and they dance, Wellington with a well-dressed lady. Then enter General Henry Percy

Percy: General Wellington. May I take you aside for a moment?

Wellington: This is hardly the best of times. May it wait until the dancing concludes? *(Twirls lady around)*

Percy: Forgive me, sire, but this is extremely urgent. It cannot wait.

Wellington: *(Sighs)* Very well, General Percy. Forgive me, madam. *(Hastily)* Don't stop on account of my absence, gentlemen. *(They go aside)* What news do you bear?

Percy: We have just received a dispatch about this ghost French army of yours.

Wellington: I see. What …?

Percy: It is not fictitious.

Wellington: *(Lowering voice)* What in God's name are you talking about?

Percy: *(Grim)* The skirmishers you sent out earlier returned. There is indeed an army and it is indeed heading for Brussels.

Wellington: *(Curses under breath)* I didn't say so but I indeed hoped that Prussian was a deceiver. A hope proved false, however. What does this army consist of?

Percy: As yet, no solid evidence. Their –

[A Noble approaches]

Noble: *(in heavy Dutch accent)* Oh most honourable General Wellington, the Duchess asks I bring you this way. She requests you sample the crab devilled eggs which I understand are –

Wellington: *(snarl)* Tell the Duchess I am, ah, currently engaged. I shall sample finger food later. *(turns away pointedly)*

Percy: I've quite lost my train of thought. *(Pauses)* Ah yes. Their camp was heavily fortified and they dared not risk detection in broad daylight. However, they heard mention from a sentry of a large number of artillery batteries and the presence of the Imperial Guard.

Wellington: Dammit! The Guard goes where Bonaparte goes. And that man has his artillery, as always. *(Amazed, shakes head)* How in the name of God could they have assembled an army so fast without our knowledge?

[Enter General Thomas Picton, covered in blood. Music stops abruptly. Everyone stares at Picton. Loud muttering in background]

Murmur in background: That gentleman has spoiled the dancing.

Picton: *(Bows before Wellington. Out of breath, wildly gesticulating)* General! Your Grace! My division has just received word of a message from

Blücher. The French are near and they can see the light of their fires. They are planning an assault at dawn! The Prussians are fortified but are unlikely to hold indefinitely. Your Grace, Blücher requests word of your plans. I departed immediately with my staff but ran into some cavalry buggers! I must say —

Wellington: General Picton, please calm down! You are babbling like an infant! *(Glances around, appears to notice whole room staring at him)* Worry not, this is confidential but completely unimportant business, ladies and gentlemen. My comrade is often thus and *(with air of telling a joke)* hath been from his youth. Pray you, keep seat. The fit is momentary; upon a thought he will again be well. If much you note him, you shall offend him and extend his passion. *(Eyebrows raised, waving hand. Crowd chuckles appreciatively)* But please! Return to your gaiety, pay us no attention. *(Beckons Percy and Picton into a corner, speaks more quietly)* Very well, now I must see a map before doing anything.

Picton: I brought one along. *(Pulls out map that is projected for audience)* Now, Ligny is here. Could the Emperor's plan be to capture there, then regroup his forces and assault Brussels?

Wellington: *(puzzled)* No ... No. That can't be right. Something else is happening. Why would the bloody Frog focus on Ligny? It's a very small town that isn't anywhere near Brussels; in fact, it's nearer the Prussian border, look. No, the only reason he would go there would be to dislodge the Prussians. But if they've advanced this far without detection, presumably they know of the way our army isn't condensed and is therefore extremely weak. But why would he just demonstrate to us where he is and give us time to prepare defences? Could it be possible his army is in two sections and can therefore launch two simultaneous attacks?

Percy: Two French armies hitherto undiscovered? Come now, your Grace, that is a bit ... *(Moves hands, searches for words)*

Wellington: *(Quietly, bordering on discernible whisper)* By God, Napoleon has humbugged me.

Picton: It makes sense! That's his plan, same as always! Attack both at once, stop us doing the same. Many old soldiers re-enlisted under King Louis XVIII during his short-lived reign and plenty of new volunteers would have joined Bonaparte –

Wellington: *(snarl, suddenly furious)* I couldn't give a damn about the French fixation with Bonaparte, Thomas! For all intents and purposes, this bugger that crawled out of his pit for the first time in eleven months is presently leading at least one enormous army straight through Belgium soil, without our knowledge until today while our forces are spread halfway across the goddamn CONTINENT! It defies any rule of war ever written, even his own! *(Petty, almost childish)* It … It's not fair.

Picton: The situation is dire, sir, but getting snappish at us shall not help in any way, with all due respect. Nor will classifying the situation in terms of 'fairness'. Were the situation fair, we would be back in London now, not in a foreign land. Were the situation fair, Bonaparte would have kept himself to himself on Elba. Were the situation *fair*, we would not be discussing fairness now!

Wellington: *(breathing heavily)* Yes … I apologise. Suppose we are right and he has divided his army. Whom would he trust with such a paramount task?

Picton: What about Marshal Ney? Bonaparte could quite easily have delegated him such an undertaking. They achieved the impossible in Russia together for a very long time.

Wellington: What did Ney's reaction to Napoleon's return appear to be?

Percy: From what information we've managed to glean, Ney was ordered to lead an army to either kill or apprehend Bonaparte when he returned from Elba. However, when he was sighted, the Monster somehow turned the tables and inspired his entire army to his cause. Though I'm certain Ney privately disliked this, he surrendered his sword and allowed Bonaparte to take overall command again. It was partially on his suggestion that he abdicate in the first place, bear in mind. Ney is a true militarist; he serves France. He has never shown loyalty toward one specific leader.

Wellington: I suppose I must commend the bugger for that. *(Desperately)* Is there any way at all this can be turned to our advantage, in your opinions?

Picton: *(Shakes head slowly)* Ney is not quite as competent a military leader as Bonaparte but just as ambitious and abhorrent. There's no way in hell he'll back down unless either defeated in battle or ordered by the Emperor directly. No matter how you look at it, your Grace, we have to engage them.

Percy: *(Quietly)* In all realism, your Grace, we may actually have a slight advantage in that Ney and Bonaparte's forces are separated. If they should join, they will quite literally annihilate us.

Wellington: Let's say we assume we're right about all this. If we are, the only liable target of Ney's would be the crossroads at Quatre Bras. They can't get to Brussels without somehow going around us, and the French never were buggers for stealth. Besides, I personally feel Napoleon himself would insist on leading that siege. However … Quatre Bras. It's an incredibly strategic position.

Percy: We may be mistaken, your Grace. Perhaps –

Wellington: No, it's Quatre Bras, it must be! For one thing, it's on the main Brussels road. Secondly, that crossroads is the route for our supplies. Food, gunpowder, medical supplies, everything … it's all brought down that road. Should it fall, we may as well consider ourselves under siege. We must fight for that place, gentlemen, and either win or die fighting!

Percy: Sire, no doubt Ney's army is not as large or as formidable as the Emperor's, but they will almost certainly still outnumber and outgun the forces we have in Belgium.

Wellington: Henry, send word to the Earl of Uxbridge. He is currently leading the Union and Household brigades to assist Blücher. Somehow they'll have to do without – we need them back here right away. Go now.

Percy: Yes sir.

[Exit Percy]

Wellington: Thomas, go see the Prince of Orange. Quite frankly, I'd rather not rely on the Dutch but they do have a reasonably sized army. Send him to me. Also fetch whoever leads that miserable

Belgian army. We need their assistance too. Lastly, find Major Bentley and Sergeant Frederick. They were instructed by Orange to attend.

[Exit Picton]

Wellington: *(Addressing audience)* Oh, what a calamity. What in God's name are we going to do? I'm merely fooling myself by thinking we can hold the crossroads under these conditions. If France is a snake, Napoleon Bonaparte is the tongue. No matter how many times we defeat him, crush him, he merely slips out again. In Spain, he seemed unstoppable, pushing my forces aside with ease. We did however beat him back over his iced Pyrenees but any thought of it ending there was a child's daydream. All of Eastern Europe was humbled into conceding they were, in fact, French. Then the snake slithered over the motherland, toward the Russian capital, where it finally lost its momentum. It crept back on itself while more and more of its tail was removed, until it was merely the head and top of its neck. We removed the head finally, locked it away for eleven months. But the sly creature never died, merely bided his time; allowing poison to replenish in his fangs. BONAPARTE WILL NEVER AGAIN DOMINATE EUROPE. Such may not be decided tomorrow, or the next day, or next week or in a thousand and one nights; but history will, at some stage, decide on our behalf.

[Enter Prince of Orange]

Orange: Most noble Viscount Wellington, what may I –

Wellington: Duke, boy, Duke! Do you never read the news?

Orange: I wholeheartedly apologise, your Grace. Now what is the meaning of this audience? I am supposed to be dancing with the –

Wellington: As you have undoubtedly heard, however late, Napoleon Bonaparte has returned from exile. What you have undoubtedly not heard is that he invaded Belgium earlier today. Britain and Belgium require Holland's assistance to stamp out this attack.

Orange: Sir, you must understand that my nation is ill prepared for war and indeed my army is worse prepared for battle.

Wellington: Prince, around the time you were still at school, your, ah, prosperous nation was allied to France. Calling itself the Batavian Republic. Do you recall such a time?

Orange: Yes, sir, of course, but –

Wellington: What you may not recall was that it was not, per se, a republic, indeed, I daresay, almost the exact opposite. Bonaparte thundered orders from Paris, threatening annihilation if not instantly obeyed. When you were annexed by Britain and became the United Netherlands, the Frog was furious at having lost one of his backyard puppet states. Should Brussels fall at any point in the future weeks, Amsterdam will be his next objective – and he will not let it slip through his fingers again. You do not even want to entertain the notion of what the revised regime would be like, mark my words on that.

Orange: *(Pale faced)* You will have full assistance from Holland, sire. I promise you that.

Wellington: I thought as much. Goodbye.

[Exit Orange, enter Bentley]

Wellington: Major Bentley, good evening. I am afraid we have a problem. Napoleon has invaded Belgium and is headed for Quatre Bras as we speak. I have had to request help from the Prince of Orange and his army. Now *(smiles grimly)* Orange is not a competent commander and last time he led a battle he managed to cause far, far more trouble then he solved. We are going to engage the French tomorrow and, as you are the largest British representative on Orange's staff, I am delegating you the task of double-checking his orders. Irritatingly, I can't authorise you the power to veto his decisions, but if he orders something absurd, you are to come directly to me. Any questions?

Bentley: Your Grace, what exactly do you define as absurd?

Wellington: Between you and me, Major, with a lot of work and excellent mentors, the Prince might make a half-decent lieutenant or a captain, perhaps. He is certainly not fit for leading an army of any kind, let alone the only one that can repel an invasion by Napoleon. I would like you to stay with Sergeant Frederick and observe the

Prince. Do not make it obvious however, unfortunately, we need to co-operate almost perfectly with the Dutch for the duration of the war and letting my doubts on to him would be the equivalent of begging for trouble. You follow?

Bentley: Yes, sire.

Wellington: Now, make haste! We must defend Quatre Bras in the morning or die trying!

[Exeunt]

Just relax

Carol McGill

JUST RELAX, THEY TOLD ME. You'll enjoy it. You just have to let yourself go.

So here I am.

I can't breathe. I give up trying to suck in what little oxygen is left in the stuffy room and yell at my friends that I'm getting some air. I duck and dart through the crowds until I reach the door and stumble through it. The cold night catches me as soon as I step outside. It seems blissful after the stuffy hall. I edge over to a cold, damp wall and lean against it. I wish I could see the stars.

The only other people out here are the ones who smoke. I know I must look weird, standing here alone, but I don't care anymore. I watch the flare from a lighter and hope the gang will decide to go home soon.

They won't, of course.

It's so loud at these places I never hear any music, just noise, pounding against my skull, and the lights bounce off my eyes and make my brain swirl and ache. Those same lights transform the vast space with the sticky floor and nondescript walls into a prison that glows with bright colours in some corners and gleams with black in others and it's all mixed together and compressed in my head into one blinding, blaring moment of light and dark and it just makes me stand there feeling utterly confused and stupid.

But that's not what you're supposed to do here, is it? Here you're supposed to have fun. You're supposed to mingle with the mass of twisting bodies and you're supposed to do what they're doing. You have to find people to imitate because you know that any move you attempt will just look idiotic. You have to stand in the sticky air with the tang of perfume and sweat and worse burning your nose and force a smile onto your face and look like it's the best place in the world to be.

And I don't even have the heart to be sarcastic or irritable about it, because I just feel so miserable and out of place, like I'm that one jigsaw piece that not only won't fit in with the rest of the puzzle, but turns out to be in completely the wrong box.

I've never understood the appeal of being in that environment, where it's too fast and too loud and too hot and too bright and too dark all at once. It only ever makes me feel slightly sick and really I just want to be at home, where it's safe, or reading a book or watching some random movie or doing anything, really, rather than be there.

But I get put in this social situation, and the worst part of all is worrying about what they'll think when my awkwardness is tangible and people stop and look at me and laugh and say, 'Just relax!'

I take a last deep breath, enjoying for one final moment the cold smoky air that can't be had inside, because I know I'll only last ten minutes max before I can't stand it anymore and I come back out here and begin this whole routine again. I look up at the sky and realise the clouds have shifted, and that up in the heavens I can see some stars.

Then I return to the door with my jaw set and I go back inside and feel the music pounding through my chest once again.

❧

Mistaken

SAMUEL H. DOYLE

There. Look!
Yes, you see her
Finally a friend you know.
A buoyant stride closing in
On the savouring prize.

That hair you remember,
Long and sinuous, an inky shade
Reminding you of blackberries,
The ones we shared last year.

Reaching for her shoulder,
Sheer delight, the tanned collarbone
Identical to that in your dreams.

She turns effortlessly,
And says ...

'Do I know you?'

Eve

Sean Ceroni

SHE SITS ON THE RED chair in the dressing room. She stares at the mirror. She loathes the image in it. She feels ugly even though she has spent the day walking down runways. She feels fat even though her stomach shrieks from under her white Chanel dress. She opens a drawer of the dressing table. She removes a small red velvet box. She gently clicks open the silver clasp on the box. It is full of white powder.

Her name is Eve.

She pours some white powder onto the table using a small silver spoon. It is her grandmother's. She gave Eve all her silverware. Seashells are lovingly carved into it. It is now covered with tiny white crystals. Eve fishes a 100 euro note and a credit card from her purse. Using the card she taps the crystals into a neat line. She rolls the 100 euro note tight, and places it gently into her left nostril.

She moves slowly over the line, inhaling every last crystal into her system.

She straightens up. She clears up all signs of her habit before placing the velvet box back in the drawer and rushing out of the room. The corridor is brimming with busybodies. Members of staff jostle by her. 'Eve, you're needed now for makeup!' is shouted at her from down the corridor. She hurries towards the makeup area, where she is grasped and pushed into a chair. She is quickly plastered with various substances before being gestured forth for final inspection by Karl Lagerfeld. He looks her up and down quickly. She can't see his eyes from beneath his sunglasses. He adjusts the positioning of the dress on her shoulders and pushes her towards the catwalk. She is hit by the bright lights of a thousand cameras. She has done this thousands of times, a thousand times too many.

She collapses onto the catwalk, her white dress billowing behind her. She can feel the flashes of camera light on her eyelids as the photographers rush onto the catwalk. It is the last thing she will ever feel.

Even This Much Chocolate Couldn't Make Us Sweet

A CLASS EFFORT

Challenge: Describe chocolate in one sentence, without reference to taste.

CHOCOLATE MELTS IN YOUR MOUTH then slides down your throat like medicine for the soul until it fills your stomach with regret.

> *The sound of a vibrating bass string, dipped in liquid gold.*

It creates an instant sweetness and tingles in a person's mouth; it brings relief to those who feel fear, illness, despair or simply addiction, it is a joyous substance that is magical and comes in many different forms.

> *A thick solid that will melt on touch and coat every part of your being in smiles.*

Imagine you've never slept your entire life; everyone always talks of how glorious it is but you don't give it too much thought, you convince yourself it's fine and that you're losing nothing and that the extra productivity is worth the constant restlessness and the feeling of hot sand in the throat – with all of this, chocolate is falling asleep in someone else's arms.

> *Chocolate is like empty words of velvet that let you down after you hear them.*

It starts as a small block of solid joy and wonder, before melting into a pool of liquid comfort and warm coziness that slowly coats your whole mouth in a layer of love.

> *If it were sound, a harmony that builds to cacophonous crescendo of sweet, silky and rich.*

My Prison

HANNAH-ROSE MANNING

I STARE AT THE WHITEWASHED wall, wondering when my life will begin. This room encloses me, trapping me in a prison of despair. I sigh heavily, hot tears running down my already stained cheeks. Nothing to do, nothing to see and no one to talk to. I run my slender fingers through my hair until its silkiness soothes me. Every day like the one before. Waiting for someone, anyone. Even my parents would do at this stage, despite their abandonment. She said my 'isolation to think about what I have done' would be temporary. Day 16 and counting. No more, no less. I keep a record of the date so I won't lose the parts of my mind that are still intact. Every day, the desperation increases. Every day, I realise what I do not have anymore. Every day, I forget why I did it and then I remember his eyes. The eyes that saw into my soul, past my prickly exterior. I hope he knows what I did for him.

The days grow longer. Each day takes a little bit of me and I see no way to get it back. I try not to wallow in self-pity, but the difficulty of trying *not* to do something overcomes me. I do not have long to live, I think. Not like this. I have no food now and scarce amounts of water. I dream of him coming to rescue me, yet I know the truth. He left and nothing can change that, not my letters, not my pleas, not my hopes, not my dreams. A few short weeks ago he held me as though he would never let me go. I felt beautiful, loved. Now look at me. A 16-year-old girl so thin her bones are showing locked up in a room with no windows or doors. Whenever I hear footsteps I think it is her. I imagine her pitying me and giving me back the one thing I want above everything else: freedom.

I try to find things to occupy my day, but the room is bare and bleak and does not accommodate the residence of humans. Every day I draw pictures on the walls but every night while I am asleep she washes them off. I cry a lot which takes up time. I hope she hears my tears, I hope she knows what she did to me. At twelve o'clock

I run around the tiny room fifteen times. I eat whatever will not kill me and I drink whatever water there is. I clean and clean and clean with an old rag until my hands are raw and filthy but the room is fairly respectable. I sing until I cannot sing any longer and I shout nonsensical words to entertain myself.

I talk to myself and to him. I answer back, but he never does. I know that he is long gone, but he will always be in my memories. I miss him every second of every hour of every minute of every day. Yet the sun keeps shining, although he is gone. The world keeps moving, although I am gone.

Heels against the Cobblestone
An Interlude

SEAN CERONI

IN 1960S FLORENCE, IN A café with green shutters, tucked away in a maze of cobblestone, a man sat enjoying a coffee. His name was Samuel Broesman. He is one of our protagonists.

Samuel was not an interesting man. He was head of Cadillac's Italian branch and was at that moment enjoying a break from a dull business meeting. He was just one more rich American among the seemingly millions who plagued the city. He was 46 years of age and he looked well for his age, with a full head of dark, slick black hair and the odd wrinkle. He wore a plain gold ring on the fourth finger of his left hand.

At this particular point in the endless sea of forgotten memories, Sam was sitting comfortably at a table outside the café, bathed in sun, drinking an espresso and smoking a cigarette. It was a busy day in Florence; the summer had brought the usual floods of tourists to its narrow streets. Sam had escaped the crowds and cameras to this café in the back streets of the ancient city centre. The only sounds were the occasional hum of a vespa in the distance and the soft cooing of pigeons flying above. It was in this silence that he heard her approaching – the rhythmic sound of heels tapping against the cobblestone. Sam could not help but stare at her as she emerged from behind the street corner. She was pencil-thin with a lithe, boyish quality to her body. She wore a baby blue velvet dress that ended very high on her thighs and chunky blue plastic boots. There was a small white (presumably faux) fur draped over her small shoulders. The icing on the cake had to be the massive pair of sunglasses that dominated her face. The blue frames curved into the grooves of her cheekbones ending with cat-eye points at the corners. She had sharp but delicate features and pale skin that distinguished her as foreign. Her hair was styled in a blonde pixie cut. She was the most beautiful woman Sam had ever seen. She is our second protagonist.

She went by the name of Cece. No one was sure of her origins but she sounded vaguely British with a somewhat aristocratic tone. She was one of those people who seemed to have always lived in Florence, forever playing the role of the mysterious socialite. She earned her keep as some form of a call girl, with the occasional modelling job. She had always wanted to die alone.

Cece noticed him the moment she rounded the corner. It was hard not to. He was the striking type. With his dark eyes and expensive suit. He looked elegant as he sat there, cigarette in one hand, coffee in the other, smoke gently drifting from his lips as he lifted his espresso cup. She hadn't set out for coffee but she wanted to observe him a little more. She walked up to the counter with a slight nuance of moxie in her steps. She noted that he was looking at her the entire time. She leaned against the counter, and in velvet tones said, 'Espresso per piacere.'

'Certo,' was the waiter's reply. She strolled out again and sank into a chair at a table directly next to Sam's. When she removed her sunglasses, they revealed huge, grey, doll-like eyes framed in thick eyeliner. She grasped a pack of cigarettes out of her bag with her long blue pointed nails and rested the pack on the table. She considered getting her lighter but thought better of it.

'Do you have a light?' she asked Sam, presuming he was of English-speaking origin.

'Naturally,' he said in the tones of a man who smoked heavily. He produced a lighter from his inside pocket and leaned towards her.

Cece leaned in, cigarette between her lips, until the lighter was directly under the cigarette. With a flick of Sam's thumb the flame burst into life and lit the cigarette. Cece and Sam leaned back and the first hurdle to a human bond had been overcome.

'You come here much?' Sam said, looking up at her.

She gave him a wry smile as smoke swirled from her nostrils before she replied with a simple 'No,' her eyes boring into his soul. 'I had a hunch the coffee would be good,' she said before emitting a throaty laugh.

'So is it appropriate to ask your name yet?' Sam asked before taking a last drag and putting down his cigarette.

'Cece,' she said softly as the waiter arrived with her espresso. She put out the cigarette and slid a slim finger inside the cup handle, her blue nail chinking against the depth. 'You have endless eyes.' Her voice was ethereal.

'Well darling, the man you see around those eyes is called Sam.'

Cece giggled. 'You remind me of a skeleton.' She stared directly into his eyes. It was at this point that Cece normally made people uncomfortable, and before long they usually came up with an excuse to leave, but Sam didn't flinch. He returned her stare. They sat together in silence for a few minutes. Despite only knowing him for mere minutes, Cece never wanted to leave his presence.

She broke the silence by saying, 'Well Samuel darling, how about we leave now that we know simply everything about each other.'

'But you haven't paid.' Sam looked at her, rather alarmed.

'Exactly,' she said, smiling as she got out of her seat.

Sam also rose and Cece darted off around the street corner without him. Sam rushed after her as fast as he could, terrified of losing her. After coughing and spluttering for a few blocks, he found Cece standing at a street corner adjusting her makeup.

'What was that?' Sam asked as he sidled up to her, scrunching his face in the effort to breathe.

'Well, I don't want to end up in jail again, do I?'

Sam wondered what he was getting himself into.

'So where shall we go, dearest?' Cece said as she applied a final layer of lipstick and snapped her mirror shut.

'What exactly did you have in mind?'

'Let's just do something Florentine,' she said as she grabbed his hand and led him down the cobblestones.

The pair walked side by side, fingers tangled.

'Why are we doing this?' Sam said as they walked through the streets, hands linked, without any direction.

'Because we are in love,' was Cece's simple answer.

Sam wondered why he wasn't disconcerted by the statement. It just seemed right. They continued in a comfortable silence.

'Buy me ice cream,' Cece said suddenly, in an unusually soft manner for a demand, dragging Sam into an ice cream parlour packed with tourists. Cece pushed ahead of the crowds ignoring the queues and annoying many. She pressed against the counter and looked at the vast tubs of coloured creams.

'Which one you like?' the man behind the counter said in stilted English.

'Blue,' she said tapping her nail against the glass.

'What colour cone?'

'Mmmm ... I don't know. SAM!' she shouted across the shop. Sam emerged from the corner of the shop and pushed through the increasingly annoyed tourists to get to Cece. 'Sam, darling, which colour cone do you think would suit blue?'

Sam shook his head, guessing she simply wanted an ice cream to match her ensemble. 'White, I think.'

The man behind the counter didn't bother waiting to see whether Cece agreed or not, which was only sensible considering the entire room was fuming and wished them dead.

'2000 lire,' he said as he shoved the ice cream in Cece's direction.

Sam quickly threw him a note and rushed after Cece, who had already left; he found her outside experimentally licking the blue ice cream.

'This ice cream tastes like plastic,' Cece said as she scrunched her mouth up to her nose.

'Well it was expensive, so enjoy it for my sake,' Sam said, putting his arm around her.

They continued on into the streets. As strange as it sounded, Sam enjoyed the feeling of being obnoxious; it made him feel iconic.

⁓

They soon arrived at Piazza della Signoria. Cece wandered over to the fountain with the enormous statue of Neptune. She gazed into the water, a constellation of copper coins reflected in her eyes. She dumped her blue ice cream into the quivering water and ran off quickly, giggling as she went.

She sat on a bench where Sam had already settled down. She began feeding pieces of the white cone to the pigeons. The stupid birds leapt upon the white flecks, battling each other off to win what seemed to be the most precious thing in the world. She loved birds. She always felt sorry for the pigeons; they were never treated with compassion in Florence. It showed how people only seemed to care for beautiful things. She gazed at the buildings around the square, tall and foreboding, surrounding her, closing in on her and the pigeons.

Cece leapt up from the bench and said to Sam, rushed, 'We have to leave now.'

'What do you mean? What's wrong? Where do you want to go now?' Sam asked, getting up from the bench.

'How far is it to the airport?' she said as she grabbed his hand and dragged him out of the square, displacing flocks of pigeons in the process.

'What? The airport! What happened?' Sam said as she dragged him down the steep steps.

'Let's go away and never come back, that's all,' she said as she let go of his hand, rushed to the road and hailed a taxi.

Sam hurried down the steps to meet her. She hopped into the taxi, leaving the door open for Sam, and leaned in toward the driver and said, 'Aeroporto.'

Sam fell rather gracelessly into the taxi, out of breath. Cece put her head on his shoulder.

'Are you sure about this?' Sam said as he lit a cigarette.

'Yes,' Cece said, staring into space, thinking about everything and nothing.

She clutched his hand. They sat in silence, enjoying the intense feeling of bliss. Cece looked out the window; the city was getting thinner and thinner. There were more trees now.

She closed her eyes and smelled the smoke drifting around the cab.

A Wet and Foggy Season

Conor Kelleher

Fog was thick last night.
The grass was wet and boggy.
Just an accident.

I'm so sorry, Ma'am.
He was a good boy, Alfie.
Didn't deserve that.

Now, don't blame yourself.
No one's to blame here, Miss Black.
He was a young lad.

He knew the place well.
The chances were so slim, aye?
No, Ma'am, not his fault.

But not yours, neither.
Now look; there are always fights
'tween mothers and sons.

Just dealt a bad hand,
That's all. Just terrible luck.
Now look, Ma'am, now look,

You did not kill him.
Not your son, Miss Black, not you.
A mistake, mark me.

He walked by the cliffs.
The fog was thick, it was wet ...
He fell, Ma'am, he fell.

Okay? Not your fault.
An awful turn of events.
We'll all mourn with you.

Sorry, what was that?
A note? Never mind that, Ma'am.
Never you mind that.

Just let me sleep

GRACE COLLINS

I'M NOT TIRED. NOT IN the way you understand tiredness. I feel like I'm being swallowed by it. It's taking over my body, it's planted its seed in my belly, it's growing around my ribs, letting its vines coil around my legs and arms. But this isn't a beautiful flower; no, it's a cold, grey, rotting ivy that's slipping into all my nooks and crannies, slowly weakening them. Its grasp getting tighter and tighter until I eventually will snap. And then it will simply move on to another victim.

It is hard to concentrate with this tiredness; it's hard to do simple things, like walk, hold a conversation, eat, write. I seem to be in a constant state of confusion. It's like I'm missing part of my day. I seem to suddenly wake in a classroom having no idea what has happened as the last I can remember I was going to bed. And it's terrifying but I can't tell a soul.

They will pump me full, weigh me down, slap a smile on my face and send me back out if they knew. They've done that before. I'd go for endless tests. Nothing being certain, never being told what was wrong. They can't admit that I'm a mystery. And when they were finished with me I'd be sent away feeling so much worse. They will tell me I'm crazy, I'm ill, I'm broken and I'm hurting. But I'm not. I'm fine. I'm just tired.

Please, I beg of you, let me prick my finger and sleep for a thousand years. But don't let a prince's kiss come to wake me. Please turn them away. Tell them the princess is gone, beyond repair, and let me sleep and sleep and sleep until there is no more time. Even then don't wake me. Let me sleep through it and then let me fade and fade until I and everything we know of this world ceases to exist. And then I shall smile, and I shall be mended and all will be well.

⌒

If I Left

Emma Shevlin

If I left
Would you care?
Would you know?
Would it show?

If I left
Would you weep?
Would you cry?
Would I fly?

If I left
Where would I go?
Heaven bound
Or underground?

If I left
You'd all be fine.
You would not pry.
You would not die.

I've done that part.

Notes on contributors

CATHERINE BOWEN

Catherine does not (and cannot) write poetry. She works mainly in prose, and has started several novels, although has not yet found the one she wants to finish. She writes a lot of fantasy; she particularly enjoys writing tall female protagonists, because as a tall reader, she feels underrepresented. She likes sailing, but doesn't really like to swim. She likes films for children. She loves to read as much as to write.

AMY CAMPBELL

Amy is sixteen and lives in Clonakilty in Cork. She is known as a rainbow-type individual who functions entirely on glitter and plans to name her future pet unicorn Blaine. She favours muffins over croissants and naturally, if given the opportunity, two of the things she'd rescue from a house fire would be her sparkly eye shadow and peach-coloured high heels with bows on. Her hobbies include drama and skipping. She began writing when she was smaller than she is now and she enjoys writing prose.

SEAN CERONI

Sean Ceroni is fifteen years old and from Leitrim, in the north west of Ireland. He doesn't like living there as it is dull and there is nothing to do. He is interested in music, fashion and film. He likes to write thrillers, romance and crime. He would love to live in the fashion capitals of the world, Paris, Milan or Tokyo. He started writing seriously in January 2013.

GRACE COLLINS

Grace is a fifteen-year-old prose poet who is a fan of the colour yellow and soft jumpers, and is hopeless at deadlines. She likes to write on her bed, preferably with some green tea, perhaps in the company of her two dogs. Trains are her favourite mode of transport. Before doing the Anthology of Writing course, revision was a mystery to her and she had never shown her work to anyone.

Samuel H. Doyle

Samuel Harry Doyle was born in Croydon, London in 1998 (yes, the same place where the riots were a few years ago). His greatest memories of life in England are falling into the garden pond and walking to school in shorts during snowy winters. At six his family returned to the rural homeland of Ireland (just in time to miss the Celtic Tiger and hit the recession) and he now lives in the middle of Monaghan's boggy countryside, where he attends St. Macartan's College. While at CTYI he appeared in many guises including but not limited to Sam Doyle, a Dalmatian, the COW, Grim Reaper, a Chicago mobster to rival Al Capone and your friendly neighbourhood Spiderman!

Andrew Duffy

Andrew Duffy is fifteen years old and lives in Dundalk. He only started writing seriously in January 2013. He finds writing to be a good way to release his feelings. He does not like to limit his writing to one genre, preferring to be versatile in the forms and genres in which he writes. He enjoys reading and reads a lot of graphic novels. His hobbies outside of writing include going to the gym, acting and playing guitar. He is an only child, which he thinks is great with the exception of Christmas time and the holidays. He dislikes Dundalk and would love to live in London when he is older.

Caelen Feller

Once, there was nothing. Then, nothing gained an interest in knitting, and other things related to yarns.

It then made a pink woollen hat, named Kandy.

This hat's attempts at knitting were less successful, and the name that was given to the conglomeration of its work was Caelen.

He writes stuff sometimes.

Conor Kelleher

Conor doesn't really know what writing is, or what it's for, or how English works, and he's especially confused as to the exact mechanics of how he came to be trapped within this book. He likes words, pianos, music, remembering, and friends, and although he understands very little about any of these and routinely breaks them into tiny pieces, he finds he has a certain knack for using them to make people happy.

~~He may or may not actually be a Secret Yorkshire Terrier.~~

He thanks you kindly for reading.

HANNAH-ROSE MANNING
Hannah-Rose is a sixteen-year-old reader/fantasy writer who visits Florida regularly. She has been interested in writing since she was a child. She maintains a good relationship with her twenty-one-year-old brother. She likes skiing, table tennis and basketball. She enjoys writing prose and likes to read most genres. She is thinking about writing crime as well as fantasy in the future.

CAROL MCGILL
Carol is fifteen years old, and has blonde hair and green eyes.

When she isn't writing fantabulous short stories, she enjoys hockey, swimming and drama. She lived in Belgium for two years before returning to Ireland with a new outlook on life. Carol used to do archery and is not afraid to shoot an arrow at someone if they try to steal her chocolate stash. When asked what she would save in a fire, she said her entire bookshelf, so one may presume she has supreme strength.

She has been writing for as long as she can remember, and her first completed work was a picture book she sellotaped together for her sister. Carol doesn't favour any particular genre, being somewhat of a free spirit. She writes her first drafts by hand in one of her several dozen notebooks, before typing it out in Shruti, her favourite font.

ORLA MCGOVERN
Orla McGovern is a fifteen-year-old poet. She's the youngest of three and has a cat called Pepper. Orla sings and has recently started to write short stories. She likes to handwrite her work and keeps a notebook beside her bed as she'll often get ideas in the middle of the night. She's a big fan of structured poems. Orla comes from a sciencey family and finds that her writing is strange as there's no one to read it. She found workshopping very helpful and wants to continue to do it as it helped her work. Orla still isn't sure about her

future but knows she want to do something interesting with her life.

Anna Mulligan

Anna is a tea-hating Dubliner and proud of it. Anna enjoys writing poetry, flash fiction, monologues, screenplays, short stories and novels. When not writing in all these media, Anna spends her time watching films, playing the piano and surfing the internet. If Anna were an animal she would be an owl and she will never entertain thoughts of living outside a city.

Hannah O'Boyle

Hannah O'Boyle is a sixteen-year-old, brown-eyed girl from Leitrim.

She regularly teaches the class to dance, as she knows ballet, modern dance, tap dance, jazz and hip-hop.

Her favourite colour is yellow and she started writing poetry as a young, misunderstood girl.

She has bi-coloured hair and enjoys long walks on the beach, stealing fake casino money and crying while reading Marianna Paige's poetry on Tumblr.

Emma Shevlin

Emma Shevlin is a sixteen-year-old from Louth who likes teenage romance novels, dinner and a show.

Standing at a perfect 5 ft 5, she has bi-coloured hair and stunning grey eyes. She enjoys wearing fake glasses to trick people about her eyesight. She started writing poetry after she broke up with her boyfriend, as it was less violent than throwing bricks through windows. Her favourite quotation is, 'This too shall pass.'

Cahal Sweeney

Cathal/Cahal/Sheldon (take your pick) was born in Chicago but has lived in Ireland since he was three. He has always liked writing and reading but only got into writing drama when he was fourteen. He lives in Drogheda with his family and four pets but hates it and wants to move literally anywhere else. He is hoping to study either Drama or History in college.